D0055548

THUNDER ON THE MOUNTAIN

THUNDER ON THE MOUNTAIN

Giff Cheshire

GUNSMOKE

First published in the UK by Remploy

This hardback edition 2009
by BBC Audiobooks Ltd
by arrangement with
Golden West Literary Agency

ISBN 978 1 405 68268 8

British Library Cataloguing in Publication Data available.

Printed and bound in Great Britain by
CPI Antony Rowe, Chippenham and Eastbourne

Giff Cheshire was born in 1905 on a homestead in Cheshire, Oregon. The county was named for his grandfather who had crossed the plains in 1852 by wagon from Tennessee, and the homestead was the same one his grandfather had claimed upon his arrival. Cheshire's early life was colored by the atmosphere of the Old West which in the first decade of the century had not yet been modified by the automobile. He attended public schools in Junction City and, following high school, enlisted in the U.S. Marine Corps and saw duty in Central America. In 1929 he came to the Portland area in Oregon and from 1929 to 1943 worked for the U.S. Corps of Engineers. By 1944, after moving to Beaverton, Oregon, he found he could make a living writing Western and North-Western short fiction for the magazine market, and presently stories under the byline Giff Cheshire began appearing in *Lariat Story Magazine*, *Dime Western*, and *North-West Romances*. His short story *Strangers in the Evening* won the Zane Grey Award in 1949. Cheshire's Western fiction was characterized from the beginning by a wider historical panorama of the frontier than just cattle ranching and frequently the settings for his later novels are in his native Oregon. *Thunder on the Mountain* (1960) focuses on Chief Joseph and the Nez Perce War, while *Wenatchee Bend* (1966) and *A Mighty Big River* (1967) are among his best-known titles. However, his novels as Chad Merriman for Fawcett Gold Medal remain among his most popular works, notable for their complex characters, expert pacing, and authentic backgrounds. A first collection of Giff Cheshire's Western stories, *Renegade River*, was published in 1997 and edited by Bill Pronzini.

CONTENTS

CHAPTER ONE

FORMULA FOR FURY

A coyote cry came off Buzzard Mountain and in a moment was echoed by another much nearer the canyon foot. Starlight fell across the four Indian chiefs who waited by Lahmotta Creek at the edge of its valley. The warning struck deeply into them, for it meant that a fateful hour had arrived.

They looked at each other questioningly. Each of these four headed a band the Indian Bureau and military classified as "non-treaties." Two of them came from the Wallowa country, the others from Salmon River. Recent events had evolved a difference of opinion among them as to their best course of action now that they had been told flatly to come or be driven in.

Young White Bird had made himself the leader and spokesman of the Salmons, and now he spoke fiercely.

"That signal was to be given only if the yellow legs threaten us. They are coming, Thunder on the Mountain. Do we fight them or run away again?"

The implication of cowardice nettled the big Wallowa he addressed. Known to the white settlers as Joseph, his strength lay in the fact that a struggle against the military forces recently gathered at Fort Lapwai would be hopeless without his people's help. So it was now his responsibility to split the confederation and render it helpless or weld it into a solid, dangerous fighting force that could at least make itself felt.

The lines about his large brown eyes, luminous in the starshine, grew deeper as he considered this. Down the creek, at some distance, the teepee camp stretched away in the thin light, erected there only that day after a move from Split Rocks, up on the prairie above this awesome canyon of the Salmon River, a maneuver he had insisted on and with which White Bird had disagreed.

Waiting restlessly, Yellow Bull of the Salmons grunted an endorsement of White Bird's question. Tuhulhutsut, medicine man of the same faction, moved his thin old body impatiently and raised his shrill voice.

"Have you no ears, Thunder on the Mountain? The soldiers are moving against us! They will be upon us when the sun comes again! We must get ready to fight them or move our village while there is still time!"

"My ears are not deaf," Joseph said with a cutting motion of his hand.

"Why do you wait?" the medicine chief said doggedly. "Have you forgotten what the agent and the one-armed soldier said? One moon we were given to give up our country and move onto their reservation! And when I rose to protest, did you not see them throw me in their jail?"

The others growled their anger at this insult from Indian Agent John B. Monteith and General Oliver Otis Howard at the last council of several that had been held at Fort Lapwai. Tuhulhutsut had spoken for the Nez Percés and told how the land had always belonged to them, how it had come down from their fathers and their fathers' fathers and how, since everything on it must remain as ordained by the Earth-Chief, it must never be sold, given away, or yielded up to force.

They had called him a nonsensical trouble-maker and clapped him in the post guardhouse until the council was over. That had done them more harm than good, for the other chiefs had refused even more stoutly to listen to their importunings and arguments. The upshot had been an explosion of the general's temper in which he had allowed thirty days for the non-treaties to come in voluntarily or be driven in by his troops.

"I have not forgotten," Joseph said.

He swung away, a tall, swift-moving man of massive frame and strong features that were strikingly handsome even for a Nez Percé. He walked down the creek toward the village, deeply troubled by the matters weighing on him this bitter night. More astute than the other chiefs, more deeply feeling, he knew it was no longer a question of holding their land by fighting or giving it up for the sake of peace. Because of the forces that had been arrayed against them, it was a choice between living as reservation prisoners or trying somehow to remain free men.

The beautiful land in question lay partly in central Idaho and partly in the northeastern corner of Oregon, a figure eight formed by two wrinkled halves pressed into the tangled mountains. The mighty Snake River and its breaks divided this figure almost equally. The eastern half was open Camas Prairie and the bordering valleys of the Salmon and Clearwater rivers, both of which were thundering streams fed by the snowy mountains.

Settlement had begun here in the early 1860s, some fifteen years before this fateful night, born of mining fever and resulting in Pierce, Elk City, Florence, and half a dozen lesser camps. Lewiston had grown up as a trading town where the Clearwater joined the Snake, Mount Idaho had developed on the southern edge of the prairie, and a few stock ranches had been established in the valleys and around the prairie. Near Lewiston was Fort Lapwai and the reservation that had already divided the big Nez Percé nation against itself, occupied by all now except the Wallowas, the Salmons, and the upper Clearwater bands.

West of the Snake lay the majestic Wallowa, Valley of the Winding Waters and ancestral home of Joseph's own band, long crowded from the west by settlers in the Grand Ronde Valley and now demanded by the government. Unlike the eastern region, it had twice been guaranteed in perpetuity to the Wallowa Nez Percés. It was excellent stock country, and the trouble was that the settlers raised cattle and horses too. What a white man wanted, Joseph reflected, he took if he could. Although his father had been alive to head the Wallowa band until five years ago, Joseph knew the story well.

In 1855 the government negotiated treaties throughout the Columbia basin, including the Yakimas, Umatillas, and others, as well as the Nez Percés. The elder Joseph and his lieutenant, Looking Glass, who still lived, had signed with the rest only because the treaty guaranteed them possession of the Wallowa and adjoining Imnaha valleys as long as grass should grow and water run. Then came the gold stampede and its wake of land-hungry settlers, and in 1863 another treaty was offered, taking away the exempted valleys too.

Because their interests were not affected, they having already accepted allotments on the reservation, the other Nez Percé chiefs had signed anew but the elder Joseph and his associates stoutly refused. Since the demand for the Wallowa was not yet pressing, no immediate effort was made to enforce the new terms on the non-signers, but the change of face left them restive and worried.

In 1872 the elder Joseph passed away, calling the son to him and reminding him of how he had always refused to yield up their ancient home. He warned that the white men were coming ever closer to the Wallowa, with their eager eyes on it as on all things else. "Never forget my dying words," he said. "This country will hold your father's bones. Never sell the bones of your father and mother."

Those words had been engraved on the new chief's heart. Pressing this way and that with influential white men, he managed to get the matter re-examined in the nation's capitol. Within a year he learned of his success, for President Grant issued an executive order again affirming the eternal right of the Wallowa Nez Percés to the valley they so loved.

Two years later, and with no explanation, that order was revoked. The cry for the Indian lands immediately became a clamorous demand, and a poaching stockman chose to hurry matters by shooting and killing a Nez Percé. Discontent ran through the Wallowas and spread to the other non-treaty bands on the Salmon and Clearwater rivers. O. O. Howard, who had been given command of the Department of the Columbia, sent two cavalry troops into the Wallowa to set up a cantonment at the juncture of the Wallowa and Grand Ronde rivers and take military possession of the valley. The showdown had come. . . .

Joseph found that he had wandered into the village while he probed his uneasy thoughts. He went on to his teepee where lay the wife who a few days earlier had been delivered of his daughter, their first child, and his twelve-year-old daughter by his first wife. He lifted the flap and slipped in on silent feet, but the wife, called Spring of the Year by their people, was not asleep.

"I heard the call from the mountain," she said quietly. "Are the soldiers coming?"

"Yes. How is the little one?"

The woman in the blankets laughed softly. "War is not for

her, and she sleeps. Are you sorry she is not a son instead of
another daughter?"

"There will be a son."

"That is a promise I make you."

His heart swelled, then grew heavier than ever. He turned
and went out into the night and heard the waters of Lahmotta running. What legacy would he leave such a son,
bones buried on a reservation so crowded and impoverished
only the weak treaty Indians could abide it? The alternative
was a war they could not hope to win. The non-treaties
totaled eight hundred people, with less than a fourth of them
effective fighters.

After the thirty-day ultimatum at Fort Lapwai, the Wallowas had returned to their valley. Some of the young men
were determined to start a war at once to drive the cavalry
out of it. They had been hard to control, but Joseph's authority had held. His village and that of his half-brother
Ollicut were packed and the two bands moved down the
valley of the Imnaha to the Snake where they crossed by
bullboat into Idaho. They were moving in the general direction of the reservation but only, as Joseph had decided, to a
council with the other non-treaty chiefs. This was to be held
at the ancient campground at Split Rocks, on the southern
edge of Camas Prairie.

That council had been even stormier than the one with
the white men at Lapwai. Looking Glass was there with his
Clearwater band as well as White Bird, Yellow Bull, and
Tuhulhutsut and their people. The Salmons were for prompt
and total war. The oldest of the chiefs and grown wise with
his years, Looking Glass smarted with them at the indignities
and injustices they had all suffered. Yet he shared Joseph's
conviction that further resistance could only compound the
tragedy of their people. Then three of White Bird's young

warriors walked boldly to the council fire, full of excitement and importance.

"Why do you sit and talk like old women?" they demanded, their dark eyes shining. "The war has begun already."

They had seen to it, with the help of hotblooded companions. Fearing that they would be led to the reservation they detested, they had made up a war party and raided down the Salmon Valley, killing several white men they had special reason to hate. The gleam in White Bird's eyes suggested that this had not been without his knowledge and consent.

The chiefs sprang to their feet and acknowledged their need of Joseph by turning to look at him. With a cutting motion of the hand he said, "You have made your war, now fight it," and strode off toward his teepee. Anger swelled his heart, for their actions had destroyed the last small hope of obtaining justice from the white men. Reprisal was bound to be swift and merciless, and they had either to fight it or try to escape. That suited the hot bloods but was a compounded disaster for the people.

Having tasted revenge, the younger warriors continued to slip away to raid on the Salmon and even on the prairie. Panic swept through the white settlements, and ranchers and their families hastened to Mount Idaho while word of the outbreak went to Fort Lapwai, sixty-five miles across the prairie.

Joseph's anger could not stand long against his feeling of brotherhood. He talked long with old Looking Glass, his father's friend, then Looking Glass took his band eastward across the prairie to the south fork of the Clearwater. At Joseph's insistence the rest moved down into the Salmon Valley to another old camping ground here at Lahmotta.

Lahmotta Canyon joined the Salmon Valley and afforded
vast reaches of fine forage for the cattle and pony herds
brought from the Wallowa. Its natural barriers kept the
weather mild, and fish were plentiful. It was a natural stronghold, cut off from Camas Prairie by Buzzard Mountain,
which could be crossed only by a long and tedious pony
trail. The warriors were well armed and supplied with
ammunition, since each summer they crossed the mountains
to eastern Montana to hunt buffalo and had expected to do
so again until this trouble came upon them. It was not necessary to run from the soldiers as yet, Joseph reflected, only to
defend the village from them. . . .

Ollicut, his half-brother and chief of the other Wallowa
band, emerged from the night. A handsome fellow, he was
round-faced and sturdy of body, and Joseph knew his heart
was torn between the fighting fury of the other young men
and his natural loyalty to Joseph. He had slipped in from the
prairie, where he had been left with a rear guard.

"The soldiers have stopped at the top of the mountain,"
he said quietly. "They are sleeping."

"How many?"

"More than a hundred."

Ollicut talked on. The day before two companies of
cavalry had reached the southern edge of the prairie, where
the rugged Salmon breaks separated it from the river canyon. They had made a forced march from Fort Lapwai and
had been joined by a force of citizens from nearby Mount
Idaho. There was a pack train, which meant that they were
prepared to stay in the field awhile.

The soldiers had started to make camp and rest after the
wearing march over the prairie, but there had been harangu-
ing from the settlers and the big command had struck on
up Buzzard Mountain in the gathering night. But the twist-

ing trail had whipped them, and when they reached the head of the canyon descending upon Lahmotta, shortly after midnight, they had been compelled to stop and rest.

Ollicut's voice was quiet, but impatience edged into it. "We could attack them where they sleep."

"No. Have the horses brought in closer. Catch and tie the best of them and have the others herded."

"We will not run——!" Ollicut broke off and moved away at an angry motion of Joseph's hand.

Joseph went back to where the other chiefs and their warriors buzzed like wasps at the foot of the mountain trail. They had talked with Ollicut and knew that the bivouacked enemy might well be surprised and destroyed. Surly, and goaded by their desire to do so, they waited for Joseph to speak, for he would be the ranking war chief if he chose to fight. Ignoring them, he took a long look at the terrain before him, well known if only dimly discerned in the starlight.

The Buzzard canyon joined that of Lahmotta at a right angle, falling down from due north. The deep V-cleft was denuded except for thin stray patches of yellow pine. The canyon scarcely widened where it broke abruptly on the Lahmotta floor, and immediately athwart it, at that point, ran a series of bare, rock-studded buttes where were buried many Nez Percés who had frequented this campground and fishery. The creek skirted the southern edge of these buttes, then ran on down to join the Salmon.

Seeming to muse aloud, Joseph said, "Ollicut will take the high ground to the right. White Bird will go up that ravine to the side to be on their flank when they come down upon us. The old chiefs will stay with me, here across their front when they turn toward the village."

"Here?" White Bird said, his voice ringing with excitement. "Do you not understand? They are sleeping and now is the time——!"

"And they are soldiers," Joseph said curtly. "It is better to let them attack us when they think we are sleeping."

"But so close to our village——!"

"The head soldier picked that place to camp and he is no fool. I have chosen this one, White Bird."

The final clash of wills had come, and it ended with the young chief subsiding. It was enough for him that the decision had been made to fight instead of running again and again from their enemies, which would be bitter medicine for the young men who were still ruled by the heats of their bodies.

The chiefs sprang away and began to organize the huddled warriors, and Joseph watched them strip to breechclouts and moccasins, preparing for battle. He heard the click of rifle bolts and saw the dark figures dissolve in the night. He heard Lahmotta and the wind's cry on the mountains. Ollicut's men came in with horses, and the best of them were left tied behind the buttes at the foot of the canyon. Joseph returned to the village and gave orders that no one was to emerge from his teepee until given permission. Then the shine of the stars faded away and dawn split wide in the sky and the fateful seventeenth of June, 1877, broke over the Salmon.

CHAPTER TWO

LIKE FISH IN A BARREL

High on the south face of Buzzard Mountain the command was in uneasy and uncomfortable bivouac, nobody getting much sleep. Crag rock and scrub timber surrounded the camp and the mountain wind rolled over it and somewhere down the long twisting trail lay trouble such as few of them had experienced, for the two troops were heavy with recruits. It had been around one in the morning when the captain gave up the slow, stumbling march and called a halt until daylight, forbidding fires for cooking, even a match to light a smoke.

For all these precautions the men not on sentry had barely shaken down when the cry of a coyote rang out and went echoing down through the canyons. Maybe only the lank scavengers of the prairies got up this high, but it was enough to make the green troops shiver in their blankets. The older men were too shot to care much, having been driven beyond their limits on a mission that had inspired them with something less than zeal in the first place.

They held a pretty low opinion of the departmental commander from Fort Vancouver who had ordered them out of Lapwai in a torrential rain just at nightfall—Companies F and H with pack train, a handful of citizen volunteers, and a squad of treaty-Indian scouts. If a few hundred other Indians didn't want to live on the reservation, they failed to see that it made a great difference. The country was big as God's hand, and if you put them on the reserve by force they would leak off and have to be run down again. Ask any leather-bottomed veteran of the reservation forts.

Yet they had been ordered to march and so they did, south over the prairie, shivering in their ponchos, and trying to sleep in the saddle. They had ridden through that storm-whipped night and until midmorning when the captain called a halt at the deserted stage station on Cottonwood Creek. There they boiled coffee and fried bacon to go with their wormy hardtack; then the sun blazed out to dry them and the ground, and they went on through a broiling day.

Around dark they reached the edge of the Salmon breaks and had been about to go into camp when some bitching settlers had harangued the captain into going on. Even their wild talk of butchered settlers, raped women, and tortured children couldn't fire the hungry, sleepy troops with enthusiasm for climbing the mountain ahead of them.

Captain David Perry, of Company F, First U. S. Cavalry, was in command by right of seniority, and he did less relaxing in that high bivouac. He was a tired man, anyway, by dint of his early middle-age and the frustrations, despairs, and deteriorations that made that time of life so hard to bear. He had been through the Modoc War, and for a brief moment had enjoyed a widespread publicity for capturing the notorious Captain Jack in the hot lava beds of northern California. Then his identity had been submerged again in the lackluster life of dreary outposts, chasing Indians, protecting settlers, and guarding roads.

Lifting the aching nape of his neck from the slick seat of his saddle, Perry looked around. His officers were stretched out about him, a little removed from the command—Captain Joel G. Trimble of Company H from Fort Walla Walla and Trimble's lieutenant, the jolly Irishman, Bill Parnell. On the other side was Albert G. Forse, his own lieutenant, and young Second Lieutenant Edward Theller of the Twenty-first Infantry who had been fool enough to volunteer for this detail and leave a young bride behind at the fort. They were all good officers, and he was especially sure of Trimble, who had been with him through the Modoc War and since. Well, he might need good officers if his hunch was right that chasing in the non-treaty Indians would be no snap.

His mind went back to the night they left Fort Lapwai in the pelting rain. He had stood on the porch at post headquarters with General Howard, who had been in and out of Lapwai for several months trying to settle the tangled Indian question. Howard had offered his one hand, which happened to be his left, and said gruffly, "Good luck, Captain, and mind you, whatever happens, you mustn't let yourself get whipped."

Surprised and irritated, Perry saluted and said curtly, "I don't think you need to worry about that, sir," and walked out into the soggy dusk to his waiting command.

He had wondered ever since why Howard had said just that in just that way. It was important, of course, that the defiant non-treaties be brought smartly to time. But on the other hand did it show on him, the inner diffidence that of late had so handicapped him?

One reason for his present unsureness was that he was wholly unfamiliar with the country ahead of him. That made him dependent on the volunteers from Mount Idaho, whom Ad Chapman commanded, and he didn't much care for Chapman who was loud-mouthed, egotistical, and carping. When he joined the command on the north side of the mountain, Chapman, who was married to a Umatilla woman, had launched a tirade over their delay in getting to the scene of the outbreak. The Indians, he said, were going to get away from them and go unpunished for their bloody butchery—which seemed pretty vindictive coming from a squaw man. He and his comrades had kept nagging until Perry had agreed to push on at once, in spite of his exhausted command. It remained to be seen how eager that homespun bunch would be for a fight when they found it.

A voice spoke in a whisper on his left, and Joel Trimble said, "Worried, Dave?"

"I don't know. Think I should be?"

"We all should be. I think that blowhard Chapman is dead wrong about them running from us like scalded cats. He makes me nervous."

"Well, he knows them and the country, so we've got to have him."

Trimble let out a sigh. "Hell, I wish we could smoke. They know we're here."

"Probably. But if we go on the assumption that they don't we just could surprise them."

"Want to bet we don't get the surprise?"

"I don't."

The first sergeants aroused the command at dawn. The horses were brought in and saddled, the packs were lashed to the mules, and the men made a cold, grumpy breakfast. Ad Chapman came over and motioned impatiently toward the treaty-Nez Percé scouts.

"I wouldn't rely on 'em," he said. "None of them bastards can be trusted a inch, no matter what they claim. You better let me and the boys lead the way."

"I'd so intended," Perry said stiffly and regretted the necessity for that. "But give me the picture, will you?"

Chapman hunkered and used a short stick to draw a few lines on the earth. "We're up here and the trail goes skally-hootin' down, twisty as hell like it was comin' up. It hits Lahmotta Creek a couple miles above the Salmon. They'll be camped down a ways, likely, and if we can get off the mountain quick and quiet we ought to catch 'em asleep. All Injuns is late-abeds."

"You ought to know, Ad," a listening settler said. "You been in bed with plenty."

"I know 'em, and I could lick any five of 'em with one hand tied. If you're set, Cap'n, let's get after the varmints."

Orders passed quietly along the forming line and the command snaked out down the trail. Full of self-importance, Chapman rode at some distance ahead, the other volunteers strung out behind him. Perry followed, the bugler beside him, then came F Troop followed by the pack train, and then Trimble's company. The trail descended in a series of elbows, from each of which a considerable sweep of the country could be seen but nothing as yet of Lahmotta Canyon. Again and again the men caught sight of the Seven Devils, rearing far to the south, and occasionally they could see a snow peak of the Bitterroots.

Without warning they came around one of the zigzags to see far below them the meadow and low buttes of Lahmotta Canyon. The Indian lodges were in plain sight along the creek farther down. A careful inspection through field glasses showed Perry no sign of life, which was in keeping with what Chapman had said about their late sleeping habits.

"What'd I tell you?" the volunteer said scornfully. "They got no idea we're within miles of this country. It'll be like shootin' fish in a barrel."

"I think we'd better scout it," Perry said.

"And tip 'em off? Dogs, you know. They got 'em by the thousands."

As yet no uneasy dogs were in evidence, and the command went on and came to a point where the tortuous trail

climbed the right slope of the canyon to a backbone that it
followed thereafter. A good half of the mounts had grown
so footsore that their riders had to dismount and lead them.
Most of the recruits loosened the cinches of their saddles
hoping to restore their animals more quickly to riding condition.

The foreground grew broken and the ridge the command
followed rose and fell, skirted on one side by the main
canyon that had brought them off the mountain and on the
other by a shallow draw. They began to climb for a distance, coming to a flat that slid up and around a rocky high
point and, on beyond this, great rocks formed a necklace
joining a series of low buttes.

Perry took all this in with a feeling of uneasiness, while
from the forward silence came the *qoh–qoh!* of a raven.
It sounded like a warning or command, but Chapman and
his volunteers kept on, paying no attention. Perry looked
back to see the main column filing onto the flat below the
stony butte, that was now on his right, and then the world
blew up.

The first volley of rifle fire took Johnny Jones, the bugler,
out of the saddle dead. The volunteers whirled their horses
while a hundred hostile rifles ripped a murdering fire into
the main command. Perry yelled to his trumpeter only to
remember he no longer had one and shouted the order to
pull back. Chapman didn't wait for that, wheeling his horse
and sending it streaking into the lefthand draw and across
to a high point beyond, his citizen soldiers riding his heels
all the way.

Perry galloped back to the milling command, bullets
blistering the air about him, dust boiling from the bedlam
scraping of hoofs and boots. The junior officers rapped their
own orders and seasoned non-coms carried them out. Troop-

ers lay dead or wounded in the dust, but horse-holders fell back with the mounts. Somebody wheeled the pack train and got it out of the way and a line formed, facing the rocky butte above the flat whence came a steady storm of death. Cavalry carbines began to retort finally, but Perry knew they were in a damned tough spot.

He remained cool, as did his officers, and they got the command formed into a stable skirmish line strung across the flat with the shallow draw on its rear. Beyond the draw Chapman had forted up with his men and was shooting over the command at the Indian-occupied butte, situated about as far from it as he could get.

Perry was considering the possibility of driving the hostiles off the butte when the necklace of rocks along the lower buttes to his left belched fire. It was as bristling as the shooting from the butte and enfiladed his whole line. Men died in their hastily built rifle pits or were knocked out of action by wounds, and Perry shouted against the whacking of guns until he had pulled the line around so its left end fronted the new attack.

The sun climbed and grew blazing hot, and the field was wholly bare except for rock and dry, wispy grass. The men worked their carbines, now and then cursed a stuck shell, and when they could they sucked at their warm canteens. No one in the line could look right or left without seeing a casualty, but rarely did anyone see skin or feather of an Indian at which to shoot. Yet bullets came out of the rocks as if blown on a wind, and troopers kept letting out that grunting, bewildered cry of impact.

Howard's admonishment, "Whatever happens, you mustn't let yourself get whipped," streamed through Perry's mind, and he knew he was worse than whipped, that he was probably going to be wiped out. On the heels of this ad-

mission came a third stunning development. Mounted Indians, twenty or thirty in number, came charging up the
shallow draw on his left and rear, again flanking him.

He tried to shout across to Chapman, who was in position
to stop them if he had the courage to hold his ground. His
yells were drowned in the uproar, but the volunteers saw
the charge coming and wheeled toward it, sending a crackling fire into the draw. The warriors didn't waver, but turned
their attention on the volunteers as they came on, clinging
to the sides and shooting under the necks of their ponies.
The volunteers broke and raced for their own mounts.

After that it was hopeless. The mounted warriors slid off
their ponies and came scrambling up the side of the draw,
well covered by the Indians hidden in the rocks. Perry
shouted himself hoarse trying to throw men across to face
them but it was too late. The regulars saw the fleeing volunteers, and Perry knew he was to be denied even a hero's
death like Custer's, for a general rout was on and the hooting
of the Indians rolled up the blood-red sky. Shouting and
cursing officers were ignored as the men bolted toward the
horse-holders, and swelling clouds of dust replaced the
smoke of gunpowder.

More mounted Indians boiled out of the rocks along the
lefthand buttes. Some of the troopers reached their horses to
be reminded that they had left them with loosened cinches.
Perry and his officers kept trying to form a rear guard so they
could get the pack train away, less for the rations than to
keep the extra ammunition from falling into hostile hands.
Some of the seasoned troopers responded, and the Irish
Parnell got the mules moving. But by then the mounted Indians, coming from down the canyon, were upon them.

The action separated into a series of swirling eddies in
which the strong and weak were quickly sorted. In places

there was hand to hand fighting, and Parnell got the pack string started while Forse covered his rear. Troopers swept past them in panic with Indians hard behind. Some of the recruits had lost their horses in the melee of trying to get mounted and went stumbling along on foot.

Half a dozen of these blundered into a cul-de-sac, a dead-end transverse canyon from which there was no escape. Young Edward Theller saw their predicament and rallied some other mounted men to fight a rear guard action while the trapped men got away. He was too late and died with the rest, widowing the young bride he had left at Fort Lapwai to volunteer for this expedition.

Presently the last of the troopers had cleared out of the dust mantling the open flat, and the Indians pursued them into the canyon. It became a race. Twice Perry succeeded in forming a rear guard and twice he was driven on. Parnell shot a closely pursuing Indian with the last cartridge in his revolver and managed to knock him off his pony, although the Indian scrambled away. Soon they noticed a war party streaking along a parallel ridge trying to flank or head them off.

Somebody wheeled and yelled at the hostiles, "Come on, you sons of bitches!" but there were not enough of his kind and he was swept on. Most of the running, dismounted men got a lift behind some comrade, and the Indians on the other backbone pulled abreast and began to send needling shots across the canyon. Then the trail dropped down into the canyon and this was stopped, but there were still Indians coming like shrieking devils behind.

Somehow the demoralized command reached the summit of the mountain, with the Indians still on their heels, and the hostiles harried them down the mountain to within four miles of the little settlement of Grangeville. David Perry rode in dismay that was soon to harden into bitterness. A third of the men he had taken out of Fort Lapwai had been left behind forever. He had made himself outstanding again, would once more have headlines, but this time it would be in galling ignominy.

CHAPTER THREE

SOJOURN BY THE RIVER

The June sun blazed, and the Indians cleaned up the battle-ground, collecting sixty-three carbines, a lesser number of revolvers, and considerable ammunition. They counted the dead soldiers bloating in the heat, thirty-three in all, and marveled that none of their own had been killed although three were wounded. Joseph packed the Wallowa camp and moved down the canyon to Salmon River. There he set his people to making skin boats to ferry to the other, less vulnerable side, brushing away the praise showered on him by the younger chiefs and warriors.

They had not only outfought a larger force than their own, they had put it to rout; and this was heady stuff that came about only because of the keen, intuitive fighting skill of their war chief. No longer did the heads of the other bands needle Joseph or argue against his judgment, although some of them now felt capable of taking on the entire United States Army. Soon they were to discover that their success at Lahmotta had had a similar effect on other Indians, not only on the Lapwai reservation but among those who were sometimes on the allotments and again off somewhere else.

Two days were spent bending green-willow frames to convert dressed buffalo hides into ferries, and while this went on a hunting party returned from Montana and joined forces with the victorious hostiles instead of going back to the reservation. The cattle and most of the 2500 ponies, brought from the Wallowa and picked up in the recent raids,

were across the river already, and the remaining horses
swam the swift current and were driven on to the grassy
hilltops. As bullboats were made ready they were loaded and
sent over, oldsters and youngsters riding atop the packs, two
or three ponies towing, and a man or so swimming at the
sides to steady the crude but efficient craft.

Joseph sent a subchief and some warriors back to Split
Rocks, at the southern edge of the prairie, to watch for more
soldiers, and the last of his people crossed by skin boat. He
dropped off pickets to stay by the river, then struck up the
side of a ridge that climbed a thousand feet in a third of
a mile. The new encampment was in a nearly impregnable
position that commanded the river. West of it the wild
breaks of the Salmon ran on to blend into those of Snake
River, country in which he could lose himself if the need
arose. The squaws raised the teepees and gathered fuel and
cooked dumplings of flour and beef and jerked yet more
beef. They had to prepare for whatever might lie ahead.

The hot spell ended, a cool night came, and in it Spring
of the Year spoke to her husband of something that worried
her. "You are still troubled. Why is that? You have turned
back the soldiers in disgrace. Your *wyakin* is strong, so what
is there to fear?"

Joseph had no words to tell her what disturbed him and
denied him sleep. Night after night he had searched his
mind for the reason this trouble had to be. Friendliness toward the white people had been Nez Percé tradition, starting with Lewis and Clark. A Nez Percé woman had led them
through the unexplored wilderness and she had become a
heroine of the white nation. Afterward there had been other
visitors, all receiving generous treatment. In the white men's
war with the Cayuse, Yakimas, and Spokanes, twenty years before this trouble, Nez Percés had fought at the soldiers' sides.

When, later, miners and settlers came they had been given shelter, food, and help. They had been given land and friendship, and in spite of all that the trouble came. The white men had only contempt for the Indian. What they wanted they took, be it land, cattle, horses, or Indian women. Protests were ignored by the authorities, yet if an Indian transgressed, as sometimes happened, he was beaten, shot, or hung.

"You fear we cannot go back to the Valley of Winding Waters?"

"That is certain."

"If we do not go to the reservation, then what can we do?"

He sighed. "That is what tears my heart. I had friends among the white people. They will blame me for this war, and I am not to blame. When the young men began the killing my heart was hurt. Yet when I remember all we have endured it is on fire with theirs. I want to lead them in a war that will make the white men realize we are men, the same as they are."

"You can do it."

"If I must. But I would take my people to the buffalo country without more fighting if I could, if they would leave us alone there afterward."

This humane spirit was not present in all the chiefs, and many of the warriors were again slipping away on raids led by White Bird, who was more war-bent than ever. He was a fiery, wiry man with a round face and concave nose that made him look more Irish than Indian. His eyes were small and cold as the snow peaks, and bitterness played about his mouth and governed everything he did. He was the idol of the young men and he took them slanting along the river until, from Slate Creek down to Snake River, not a settler, building, or head of livestock remained.

Yellow Bull had taken his band to camp at Horseshoe Bend, some distance up the river, while they waited for the soldiers to come after them again. He was a gawky man, sharp-featured and vain. Graying hair showed under the war bonnet he now wore, and sharp, squinting eyes rode over an eaglet's-beak nose and a thin, ruled mouth. His encampment was within an arrow's flight of Slate Creek where forty white women and children and twenty-three poorly armed men had taken refuge in a hastily built log stockade.

From a freight train on Camas Prairie, during the early raids, his warriors had captured three kegs of whisky, and more was taken from stores looted along the river. They drank and pranced and slept and sometimes went howling up to Slate Creek to brandish their rifles in mock attack on the stockade and boast of their victory at Lahmotta.

Tuhulhutsut, the medicine chief, reacted to the victory with an increased mystic fervor. For years he had been a fanatic follower and preacher of the Smohalla or Dreamer belief, a doctrine that had swept over much of the West. Its principal tenet was that the Indians should accept no change in their way of life, in return for which the Great Sky Spirit would send down a war chief to lead them in driving the white men from their valleys and hills. Maybe, he whispered to the people, Thunder on the Mountain would prove to be this leader.

Ollicut had been born of the same father as Joseph but by another woman, and possessed the striking handsomeness of Joseph. He and Looking Glass, who was now on the south fork of the Clearwater, were the closest to the war chief and the ones he most trusted. They alone shared Joseph's feeling that if war could be averted it should still be done.

The weather stayed cold, and runners came in from the Split Rocks scouts. They reported that Captain Perry was still at Grangeville, licking his wounds and trying to whip his command back into fighting trim. The Lahmotta dead remained unburied, although Chapman and his volunteers essayed to visit the battleground and look around. They didn't venture near the Indian encampment, and the river pickets left them alone. They were soon gone, and wildness came back to Lahmotta with an illusion of the old independent and peaceful life.

But at Fort Lapwai the military was making wiser and more careful plans to put a swift and bloody end to that, an accomplishment made imperative by developments Joseph knew nothing about.

In the great wheeling circle of prairie and desert that formed this section of the Columbia basin were three other reservations containing thousands of Indians as resentful of their fate as the non-treaty Nez Percés. Word reached the fort that, over on Crab Creek, Chief Moses had somehow learned of the stunning defeat of the soldiers and sent out word for a thousand warriors to join him there to go to the assistance of the valiant Nez Percés. This was also the country of Smohalla, founder of the Dreamer religion, who like Tuhulhutsut sensed in Joseph the qualities of the great war chief to be sent down to them from on high. If this force once moved it would empty every reservation in the Northwest.

Oliver Otis Howard, on whom the responsibility for meeting this devolved, was no obscure frontier army figure. During the Civil War he had commanded a division and eventually a corps in the army Sherman took wheeling through Georgia and up the Carolina coast. For several years afterward he had headed the Freedmen's Bureau in the national

capitol, and then had been an aide and eventually the re-
placement of General Crook during the Apache trouble on
the southern border.

Now he commanded the Department of the Columbia,
which embraced the state of Oregon, the Territories of
Washington and Idaho, and all of far-off Alaska. Yet for
months his attention and time had been monopolized by
this dinky little reservation fort at Lapwai, to which he had
been shuttling from Fort Vancouver trying to get the newest
Indian trouble ironed out.

Now a man of forty-six, Howard was growing heavy, and
he wore a full, wiry beard that was darker than his whiten-
ing hair. He had trained himself long since to get along
without the right arm he lost in the fighting at Seven Pines,
below Richmond, in the war that lifted him high in rank.
An austere New Englander, he lacked the dash that inspired
troops, and his natural plodding tendencies were further
complicated by an overweening piety that prompted such
things as his refusal to march his troops on the Sabbath and
his insistence on preaching to them and handing out religious
tracts.

On the heels of the shattering news of Perry's defeat and
rout came word of the convergence of the Columbia River
bands on Moses' encampment, some of them burning the
houses of settlers as they passed. But Howard had not been
idle, having already arranged for reinforcements, calling in
two more troops of the First Cavalry from the Wallowa
cantonment and ordering up four more companies of the
Twenty-first Infantry from Forts Stevens, Vancouver, and
Walla Walla, and from Sitka, Alaska.

Musing over the information that the hostiles were still
in the Salmon River country, the general perceived a
strategy that might turn the tables on Joseph as swiftly as
the war chief had turned them on him.

Calling in an aide, Howard said, "Fletcher, get off a dispatch to Major Green at Fort Boise. Tell him I want three troops of horse readied for the field. Impress the urgency on him and say detailed orders will follow." He stroked his beard with his one hand. "That just might do it."

"Yes, sir," the lieutenant said puzzledly. "May I ask what it will do?"

"I'm taking the field myself, and Green will serve as the anvil to my hammer." Rising, Howard carried his portly body to a wall map of the Territory and regarded it. After a moment he pointed. "Take a look at that, Fletcher. The country south and west of the Salmon is rugged, you observe, but there is a road that runs south up the valley and over the mountains to the open country in southern Idaho. Where, as you know, Fort Boise is located. That is the route Green's unit will follow. Now, consider."

"Yes, sir."

Howard moved his hand over the washboard mountains between Joseph's position on the Salmon and his old stomping grounds in the Wallowa Valley, some forty miles to the west. "It's pretty obvious what that wily Indian's up to. He's in a position that's well nigh impregnable, as he just demonstrated. But he can pull deeper into the mountains if he has to. They're well armed and supplied, and he could expect to hold out in that country a long while. So we've got to bring so much force against him he can't stay where he is now."

The lieutenant nodded. "You hope to drive him south into Green. But what if he goes west, back to the Wallowa?"

Howard shook his head. "He won't do that. He doesn't know I've evacuated the Wallowa cantonment and thinks there would be a force there ready for him. No, he'll go up the valley and into the Salmon Mountains, and I want Green there ahead of him."

"It ought to do the job."

"I think it will. So set it up with Green."

"At once, sir," the aide agreed.

Having settled on his retaliation, and sure it would result in a crushing defeat of the hostiles, Howard resumed his thoroughgoing and unhurried attention to details. He had L and E Troops on hand from the Wallowa, and Company B of the Twenty-first Infantry was already stationed at Fort Lapwai. He might have dispatched them to reinforce Perry at Grangeville for a much swifter blow, but he was making no more ventures without overwhelming force.

So he waited, wrote reports, and issued orders for several days, but there was hurried effort elsewhere as troops and supplies moved toward Lapwai. Snake River, the main tributary of the Columbia, was navigable by steamboats as far up as Lewiston, some ten miles west of the fort, where great quantities of military stores began to pile up and where steamers presently deposited the troops ordered from down the river.

This all moved on to Fort Lapwai and, on June the twenty-second, Howard's command of five infantry companies, two cavalry troops, and a volunteer company from Walla Walla rolled out of Lapwai and headed south across the prairie. It was accompanied by a battery of light artillery, a few treaty-Indian scouts, and on his personal staff was the general's son, Lieutenant Guy Howard. This was the hammer, a mighty one, although it was still a hundred miles from the anvil Green's force was to create for it to smash Joseph against in the Salmon Mountains.

The Indian reservation ran south of Lapwai to Craigs Mountain, a reaching eminence that stretched east to the south fork of the Clearwater. Beyond the mountain, on Cottonwood Creek, was the now deserted station known as

Cottonwood House, used by the stages to Mount Idaho, Elk City, and Florence, which the command reached on the first day's march. There, that evening, it was joined by Captain Perry who brought his bloody, dispirited command up from Grangeville.

Howard's natural kindness took the sting out of his rebuke to Perry, who was censurable mainly for failing to scout the situation into which he took his command instead of relying on Chapman. In return he got a detailed report on the battle and Joseph's move across Salmon River, afterward, and the encampment on the edge of the plateau above the river that seemed designed for permanence.

"Maybe permanence," Howard said. "How strong is he, Captain?"

"It's hard to say, sir, but he had enough, and more have joined him."

"Looking Glass went over to the Clearwater," Howard mused. "Do you think he's sending Joseph men?"

"I've seen no sign of it."

"Well, I'd say he is. He's sitting on the edge of the reservation, and I think it's leaking men too."

"That's probable, sir. God knows how many converts I made for their lost cause."

"Don't berate yourself, Captain. You fought a courageous fight in a bad situation, and I'll make that plain in my report."

"I appreciate that."

But something had happened to David Perry, and even the general knew it.

The next day was Sunday so Howard refused to march, but he did send Joel Trimble's cavalry ahead to reinforce the settlers in the Slate Creek barricade. He hoped their presence on the Salmon would sober the Indians and stop their depredations until the main command could deal with them properly.

That evening a mail rider left for Fort Lapwai, and during the night his horse came back with an empty saddle. This indication that the hostiles were not all off on the Salmon sobered the men while they cooked their morning bacon and coffee. Howard's respect for his foe went up enough that, on the twenty-fifth, he split his force and moved it by two separate routes to Johnson's ranch, above Lahmotta Creek, so as not to have all his eggs in one basket. On the day following he took the reunited command on a reconnaissance into the fateful canyon and on into the Salmon Valley beyond the battlefield.

Strongly intrenched beyond an unfordable river, the rebelling Nez Percés had been warned in advance by the return of the scouts they had sent out to Split Rocks. They did not seem awed by the reconnaissance or the horse troop that had already gone up to Slate Creek or by the main command when, on June the twenty-ninth, it moved down into the canyon and bivouacked near the mouth of Lahmotta Creek.

Howard sent a detail to bury the dead on the battlefield, but otherwise seemed in no more of a hurry than he had ever been. He wanted to be sure that Major Green had time to get his Fort Boise column in position to head off Joseph when the Indian was forced to move. He had also sent for more reinforcements, who were on the way. Since Joseph seemed to be getting recruits from Looking Glass and the reservation, he wanted the additional strength for himself. But he did begin to hunt up boats to carry the command over the river when the time came to cross.

Their first day on the Salmon passed with no more belligerence than the jeering of the Indian pickets across the river and the wholehearted return compliments of the troops.

Now and then a few shots were fired, but nobody was hurt, and once the Indians put on a demonstration, hooting and charging their ponies toward the river.

The next day reinforcements arrived in the form of Ed McConville's Lewiston and Bill Hunter's Dayton volunteers and five companies of the Fourth Artillery, who were scheduled to fight as infantry. The command had succeeded in finding enough boats here and there along the river, and they got a cable anchored on the other side and managed to keep the Indians from cutting it loose.

But the third morning Howard crawled out of his A-tent to discover that the Indians had vanished. No more pickets skulked along the far bank, no more smoke daubed the sky over the encampment, and Yellow Bull's band was reported to have left its camp at Horseshoe Bend. Bill Hunter, who was to prove himself a different breed of cat than Ad Chapman, was crossed with two of his volunteers, and they probed all the way to the top of the ridge. They returned with word that the Indians had departed in such haste they had abandoned considerable stores.

The signs showed that they had moved west, the direction Howard had been positive they would not go, and his whole strategic concept was threatened. He grew uneasy about a supply and ammunition train he had coming out from Fort Lapwai and needed badly now that he had so large a command, so he sent off Perry to escort it over the prairie. Then settlers came to report positively that a band of reservation Indians had slipped through to join Joseph, so he sent two more cavalry troops, with Gatling guns, to surprise the suspected Looking Glass and make prisoners of his band. Finally he dispatched orders to Trimble on Slate Creek to cross his troop there and join the main body on the other side.

CHAPTER FOUR

ACTION ON THE PRAIRIE

If ever an army officer had had opportunity to know and
grow to like the non-treaty Nez Percés he was Captain
Stephen G. Whipple, commanding Company L of the First
Cavalry. He had spent the past year in command of the
Wallowa cantonment with his own troop and that of his good
friend, First Lieutenant William H. Winters of Company E
who was with him now on the prairie.

"By God, I hate to do it, Bill," Whipple said to his com-
panion. They sat their saddles across the river from their
objective, which was the sleeping village of Looking Glass,
in the first streaky light of what promised to be a red-hot
day. "They've got their truth the same as we've got ours,
and I can't make myself forget it."

Winters nodded, his own eyes bleak. "You'd better forget
it, Steve, because you've got orders: surprise this village and
make prisoners of its inhabitants—and it looks to me like
we've got the surprise."

"We'll take no prisoners without a bloody fight," Whipple
said stubbornly, "and I feel for old Looking Glass. I wish I
had the general's faith in manifest destiny and all that. I'm
not so sure the lords of creation intend for us to take over
all this country and run the Indians out. They've got as much
reason to believe the gods will send a war chief to help drive
us out. Who's right?"

"Both sides, maybe," Winters said. "Right's what a man
believes it is, I guess."

"Can two rights go to war with each other?"

"See it happening, don't you?"

Whipple hardened the muscles of his weather-stained jaw. He had had this greasy feeling in his stomach ever since they were ordered over here into Idaho, but he was an officer who obeyed orders. Another look through the field glasses showed no sign of life down there, no smoke, no Indians, not even dogs, although the latter were not inclined to lie late abed. He pulled the glasses down from his eyes and frowned.

"That looks a lot like Dave Perry said the Lahmotta village looked."

"Think they've got something set for us? Maybe we'd better test it with the Gatling gun."

"No. If they're onto us, they're too smart to tip us off. If they're not, we've got a chance to overcome them before they can get ready to fight. You split your outfit and get on their flanks. When you're ready I'll take mine down into the village."

Whipple sat there a moment longer, studying the country about them. The south fork of the Clearwater came down from the Bitterroots, an outlying range of the Rockies that separated Idaho and Montana. Its valley was one of the most beautiful Whipple had seen, making a slow curve to the north along the eastern edge of the prairie. After a forced march through the night they had just come up to it, and now he turned and rode back with Winters to where their two troops of horse waited grumpily in the concealment of a wooded ground swell.

"Well, let's get it over with, Bill," Whipple said.

Winters spoke to his second lieutenants, halved his company, and the two details moved up and down the river and crossed. Watching with his binoculars, Whipple saw the

two platoons get into position to help him if he ran into
trouble, then he took his troop directly down the slope to the
ford and went splashing across. Nothing happened, and they
reached the village and went through it and still nothing
happened at all.

"There ain't a goddamned Injun around!" his first sergeant
yelled.

That seemed to be the case. Whipple called in Winters and
the united command went through the village on foot,
searching each teepee. Considerably deflated, the keyed-up
men remembered that it was for this they had made a march
of thirty air miles and gone all night without food or even
a smoke. Suddenly they wanted Indians and welcomed
Whipple's order to break into platoons and comb the sur-
rounding canyons and hills. In this search they came upon
some fifty abandoned Indian ponies, but that was all. They
returned to the village in late afternoon and burned it and
went up the river to Cottonwood Canyon and made their
own camp.

Lying in his blankets that night, Whipple felt a strange
relief that he had not been forced to subdue a village of his
old friends with gunfire. Yet only some fluke had prevented
it, and he was going to have to fight them with all the
energy he possessed before this thing was settled. Right or
wrong aside, the hostiles were not going to be shoo-ins, no
matter what the Indian Bureau and high army straps thought
about it.

He made another effort the next morning to discover some
sign of the fugitives. As nearly as he could determine, the
village, somehow warned, had simply exploded in every
direction and vanished from sight. He gave it up and headed
his command along the canyon toward the Cottonwood stage

station, which was twenty miles to the west and at its head.

There was every danger, Whipple realized, that Looking Glass, finished with playing innocent while he recruited warriors from the nearby reservation, had now gone on the warpath in earnest. That reminded the captain of the supply and ammunition train Perry was to bring out from Fort Lapwai, a prize the wily old chief might well be able to capture. He decided that instead of returning to the main command on Salmon River directly he would lend Perry a hand.

The command reached the deserted stage station the evening of July the second and bivouacked on the hill above, from which it could watch the prairie and stage road, and the very next morning Whipple's suspicions seemed to be confirmed. Word came from passing settlers that an Indian war party had been seen near Craigs Mountain at a point ten miles to the northwest. This was a strong indication that it, too, was watching the road for Perry's pack train.

Whipple ordered his two civilian scouts, Charlie Blewett and Bill Foster, to reconnoiter. Both men were young, intimately acquainted with the country, and could do a quicker, safer job of it than could the troops. The scouts struck off, and as they approached the mountain the terrain grew rougher, brushier, and while they took every precaution they had to run big risks. Yet they pressed on without seeing an Indian or knowing they were anywhere near one until, some eleven miles from the command, they were about to top out of a long draw.

The whole brushy foreground erupted in rifle fire and, riding in the lead, Blewett caught the worst of it. Foster yelled, "This is no place for us, Charlie!" and started to turn back down the draw. But Blewett decided to make an issue of it and dismounted and ran for cover. He never made it. A bullet dropped him, and his frightened horse broke away and galloped straight on toward the Indians' position. Foster made a desperate effort to head it off, but the steady shooting drove him back. So he made his own stand and called back to Blewett to get into the brush somewhere and hide.

He managed to hold his place until Blewett, wounded in the leg, limped down the creek, and disappeared into the timber. Then mounted Indians broke out of the forward cover and bore down on him, and Foster had to turn and ride for his life. The hostiles wouldn't let him circle to Blewett and kept up the pursuit to the Cottonwood station and hill before they turned back. Foster went driving on to Whipple's command to get help for the wounded scout, whom the Indians might or might not have lost track of.

When he understood what the excited scout was trying to tell him, Whipple called for ten volunteers to go ahead while he got the rest of the command started. He had the volunteers quickly, and Second Lieutenant Rains led them out, with Foster returning to guide them. The hostiles had evaporated from the prairie. Rains' detachment rode at a gallop, and the young officer made a fatal error.

Whipple had warned him to keep to the high ground so he could watch the roundabout country, but better time could be made taking it as it came. Rains did this, more or less following the stage road, and considerably short of the site of the first ambush his detail ran into another. They were near a spring, on the road and up the footslope, and the Indians were in the rocks and brush ahead of them.

The detachment took it coolly, although the men knew they were in a bad spot. Some of them dismounted and found cover in the rocks by the road while the rest, under

Rains, charged the Indian position to flush the enemy. They couldn't manage it and were driven back to join their comrades. Foster's horse was shot from under him and, trying to run on afoot, a bullet found and killed him.

Springfield carbines kicked the troopers' shoulders while more Indians swarmed up to join the attackers, pouring in from the south and west. Bullets spanged off the rocks, cutting the men's faces with splinters, and now and then they found men and killed them. A wounded man, sitting with his back against a rock and trying to fight, was shot between the eyes, and smoke rolled over them and the Indians and the crash of guns bounced from the nearby buttes.

Whipple was still five miles down the stage road when there loomed before him more armed and howling Indians than he had ever seen before, and he knew that nothing could save Rains and his men, let alone Charlie Blewett. He was compelled to reverse his badly outnumbered command and take it back to the Cottonwood hill, the only place where he could hope to save it.

The Indians, 150 strong, declined to attack the hill where he soon had his men digging rifle pits. So many hostiles on the prairie convinced him that this was not the evanescent Looking Glass alone. He had heard the rumor of the thousand warriors Chief Moses was supposed to be recruiting on far-off Crab Creek, and the chilling thought slid through his mind that this force had come from there, a prospect that meant there wouldn't be a white man, woman, or child left alive in the Lapwai military district in another fortnight. Then a new suspicion wormed into his thoughts. Joseph's whole band could somehow have escaped from between Howard's hammer and Green's anvil, and that made more sense. Joseph himself must have turned knife, sliding back on the prairie, and not only cutting Howard's communications but separating him from the supply train that by now the general would be needing badly.

The Indians contented themselves with riding wildly on the prairie, brandishing their weapons and yelling challenges, and when night came down Whipple's command slipped away to the north to meet Perry and the pack train. The next day, which happened to be a July the fourth nobody felt like celebrating, the train reached Cottonwood hill under the watching eyes of the Indians. The supplies and ammunition were a prize Howard's command needed desperately and the Indians wanted equally, and the hostiles lay siege to the hill that was now defended by three troops, a force equal in size to their own.

Southward in the Salmon breaks, twenty air miles away but much farther by trail, General O. O. Howard's command was scraping the bottom of the barrel. The commissary had started to issue horse meat, which failed to tickle anybody's palate, and the supply of hardtack, coffee, and sugar had run low. In his eagerness to retrieve the explosive situation created by Perry's defeat, the general had brought up troops much faster than supplies. There would be a number of wrinkled bellies before that was remedied.

Yet to Howard this privation was a secondary worry, for the mighty hammer he had forged here was poised to strike at something that still had not been found. It had taken two days to throw the unwieldy command over the river, and the volunteer captain, Hunter, had made a scout west to the Snake without seeing anything of Joseph's band. So Howard had sent him off to the south to see if there was any sign of Major Green, coming north from Fort Boise. Green wasn't there.

Yet Hunter raised an excitement on his return, for his outfit had come upon a large band of Indian horses and brought them in. This suggested that Joseph was still somewhere in the vicinity, and the only way to locate him was to forget Green momentarily and pick up the Indian trail. Hunter had not tried to follow it directly, instead cutting across to the known Snake River crossings to save time. Now he was told to follow it wherever it led, and the command would keep as close as possible behind.

Howard had been impressed by Hunter's volunteers, lean, hard-bitten men from the cow country around Dayton, over in Washington Territory, most of whom were seasoned frontiersmen and expert marksmen. But no great skill was needed to discover the trail of the hostiles, for Joseph had moved a great number of horses with him. The route struck off to the northwest over a wide grassy mountaintop in the general direction of Canoe Encampment, on Snake River, which again led Howard to suspect that Joseph was returning to the Wallowa.

The volunteers made good time, but the main command found it less easy going. Getting up the mountain to the high plateau was bad enough, for the sky opened and rain came down in buckets. It kept up all day and through the night, and pack mules floundered and sometimes slipped and went skidding down the mountain. The train and howitzer battery were only halfway up by dark, and the cavalry and foot troops, as well as the general, went without food and blankets until the middle of the next day.

It was night again before the command was united on a small stream across Salmon River from the mouth of Rocky Canyon, and it did not turn out to be a night of badly needed rest.

A courier from Cottonwood reached the opposite bank of the river somewhere in the early morning, identified him-

self to the pickets as Peter H. Ready, a settler, and swam
his horse across. Howard was roused from his tent and stood
with a poncho over his sleeping garments and listened to
what the exhausted man had come to tell him.

"Joseph back on the prairie?" he said in disbelief. "That's
impossible." But if it wasn't Joseph, who was it? Moses?
That possibility was even more alarming.

Pete Ready was at least positive about what had happened up there. Two scouts had been killed and Lieutenant
Rains' party wiped out. Whipple's command, now passed
to Perry, his senior, was besieged on Cottonwood hill along
with Howard's supply train, and these were all pretty vivid
facts in Ready's mind. The general accepted them, finally,
and realized that for the last few days he had chased a
will-o'-the-wisp. Joseph must have recrossed the Salmon
with his whole band, an act of unforgivable audacity that
had flanked a general of the army, cut his communications,
and threatened his whole campaign.

Whatever his failings, Howard was not one to cry over
spilled milk, and he was not the dullard the Indian made
him seem. For one thing he had commanded the field at
Gettysburg until Meade arrived to take over, and during
the rest of that bloody battle he had held a vital point on
Cemetery Ridge against Pickett's charge and all the other
hell the Johnnies could throw at him. But that was conven-
tional war, the kind a man could understand, and this was
something different.

Turning to Bill Hunter, he said, "Captain, how soon can
you and McConville be ready to go to Cottonwood?"

"I reckon we're ready now, Gen'ril," the volunteer said
promptly.

That surprised Howard enormously. "Then proceed, sir,
and good luck to you."

A hundred strong, the Dayton and Lewiston volunteers hit the river where Pete Ready had crossed, swam the boiling water, and struck up the frightful gash called Rocky Canyon that led through the eastern breaks to Camas Prairie.

Howard knew that he was in for equally hard going, himself. Possibly he could find the ford the Indians had used and get the big, awkward command across, but that was a gamble. The only sure thing was to make his way back to Lahmotta Creek, use the ferry improvised there earlier, then head for the prairie to settle it with Joseph. A methodical man, he chose the latter alternative.

The command turned back on its line of march over the open flat-top mountain and down the slick hill to Lahmotta Creek. The boats at the crossing remained unmolested, and the artillery, ammunition, and stores were ferried over. The mules were coaxed and cursed into the water, the horses following them, and the men went over, and the expedition re-assembled where it had been nearly a week earlier.

CHAPTER FIVE

CLIMAX AT COTTONWOOD

When it grew apparent that Howard meant to cross the Salmon to attack him, Joseph had made a fateful decision. The strategy was not all clear except that its objective was still not to be forced onto the reservation, and that was enough to suggest his next movement. He would feint from Lahmotta toward the Wallowa country by heading northwest toward Canoe Encampment on Snake River, an ancient ferrying point of the Indians. At the last moment he would turn north and pass over the Salmon himself, turning east thereafter to flank the puffing general and cut him off from his base at Fort Lapwai.

So the Nez Percés had accomplished in thirty-eight hours what it had taken the yellow legs three days to do, passing over broken, mountainous country with all the impedimenta of his people, the families and old men, the sick and injured, the packs and the huge stock herd. On the night Howard slept without blankets on the wet, slippery mountainside the Nez Percés were in a comfortable camp on the prairie side at Billy's Crossing where they were still based. Had Howard dared to follow directly after them instead of doubling back he would have had his contact summarily.

The young chiefs, Ollicut and White Bird, had become Joseph's field officers, leading out war parties to cut the prairie road to Lapwai and stop all couriers and take advantage of such opportunities as confronted them. They had been successful, letting the fact turn their heads even more, an indulgence Joseph refused to allow himself. He had no illusion about the outcome of a prolonged military struggle between himself and the United States. He had heard nothing about the rumbling on the other basin reservations nor of Chief Moses' recruiting. Contrary to popular suspicion he had not asked for help from anybody, relying strictly on himself and the two hundred warriors he commanded.

When his scouts reported that a courier had got through to Howard on the Salmon, Joseph knew he would soon have the one-armed wiry-beard hot on his heels again and he ordered the main camp moved to Red Rock Spring, a little northeast of the Cottonwood stage station. This was done, and the proximity to the besieged troops and supply train was only a secondary consideration. The move also placed the hostiles in a position to run east toward the Bitterroot mountains and the plains of Montana if they had to take flight again.

Yellow Bull and Tuhulhutsut helped with the tedious but necessary details of the camps and marches, which the young chiefs disdained, and, when Joseph sought their advice, the old chiefs gave him wise counsel. The women continued to dry and pack beef and the youngsters played the bone game, then word came that a large company of volunteers, under Bill Hunter, was rushing up Rocky Canyon to reinforce the surrounded soldiers on Cottonwood hill. When White Bird wanted to ambush the volunteers before they could get out of the canyon, Joseph shook his head.

"Your hot blood will carry you too far, White Bird. In two suns we have killed thirteen enemies. That is enough for now."

The young chief scowled, restive and eager to repeat the success at Lahmotta Canyon, which still ran in his veins like wine. He knew there were a hundred volunteers on the way and that the command of regulars besieged on the hill was in itself as large as the Indians' fighting force. With the volunteers to reinforce the yellow legs, capture of the supply train would be impossible, and the hostiles' own position would become precarious.

But Joseph must know that too, so White Bird said gruffly, "Then what will we do?"

"We will go east to the Clearwater."

"To join Looking Glass? The soldiers would never let us do that."

"How can they stop us when we will not be one band but two? You will take the warriors and go south by way of Split Rocks and turn east to the Clearwater bottom. If they want to fight they will follow you. I will take the village and horses and go east by way of the canyon. The soldiers are too few to follow both of us."

White Bird saw that this was good and whirled away on his pony. Soon he was moving out with most of the warriors to run head on into another of the opportunities the prairie had been presenting to him.

Like the soldiers on Cottonwood hill, Mount Idaho had celebrated Independence Day without fireworks and oratory. The town had been the refuge for the settlers who fled Camas Prairie at the outbreak of hostilities and who, with the local citizens, were now barricaded in a flimsy stockade. The military reverses had alarmed them then; now they panicked when the Indians reappeared on the prairie.

The settlement's volunteer company, when led by Ad Chapman, had precipitated the rout in Lahmotta Canyon by folding in a vital position and taking flight. Since then the volunteers had booted out the self-important Chapman, electing D. B. Randall their captain and Jim Cearley and Lew

Wilmot first and second lieutenants. In consequence this was a much more reliable military organization than before.

It was early on the morning of July the fifth when Randall heard that the Nez Percés had recrossed the Salmon, with it being a good guess that they intended to join Looking Glass on the Clearwater River. Their line of march could be by way of Split Rocks, their old camping ground, which would bring them abreast this worried little town. On the other hand, it could be a trail along the edge of Craigs Mountain, safely to the north of Mount Idaho.

Randall looked up Wilmot and told him what he had heard. "It might be a good idea, Lew," he concluded, "for you to make a scout around Lawyers Canyon."

Wilmot agreed and picked ten men, got them ready for the scout, and was about an hour out on the trail when he met Dan Crooks, a civilian packer with the supply train, whom Captain Perry had sent in for help. It was Randall's first intimation of the ambushes in which the scouts and Rains' command had been annihilated, and the fact that the Indians now stood to take the supply train was appalling, for it put Joseph one step away from ruling all of central Idaho. Wilmot reversed his detail and returned speedily to Mount Idaho, taking Crooks with him.

Randall called for fifteen more men to go on what might be a suicidal mission to help Perry. But the townsmen objected to weakening their own defenses that much, so Randall had to content himself with adding a few men to Wilmot's detail and taking out a command now numbering seventeen men himself. They hit the Cottonwood stage road in a file of pairs, on what was about a twenty-mile ride. If anyone saw the humor in this small force riding to the relief of three troops of United States Cavalry, he didn't feel like laughing about it.

The country rolled, so that only infrequently did they find themselves on ground high enough to let Charlie Johnson see the fore-country through his field glasses. They had reached a point a few miles from the stage station when Johnson espied, far to the northeast, a large band of horses moving toward the head of Cottonwood Canyon. They were handled by Indians, and the volunteers guessed correctly that Joseph was moving to the Clearwater along the northern route, which would lessen the danger to Mount Idaho. A little later they saw that the horse band was followed by a large number of Indians, with many women and children.

The command heaved a sigh of relief, and Abe Bartlett said, "Looks like Perry returned better'n the redskins could send, boys. There's no need for us to go on."

"Better make sure what's happened," Randall decided. "Them Injuns're trickier than a trainload of card sharps."

The detail rode on, its tension eased; then a rider appeared on a hill ahead of them and at some distance left of the stage road. He didn't look like a trooper, but, knowing there were civilians with Perry, one of the volunteers rode out and made a circle, the sign of recognition agreed on by the settlers at the start of hostilities.

The distant horseman executed the same maneuver, which was the adopted reply of recognition. Reassured, Randall took the command on, growing puzzled again when other horsemen were seen hurrying to join the first. He took his own look through Johnson's glasses and realized in horror that the riders up there were Indians, stripped down to fight. All at once there seemed to be a hundred of them.

A moment later, when he swept the glasses to the rear, his heart contracted again. Hidden by high ground, a second war party had flanked him and cut off his retreat to Mount Idaho. The other force stood ready to sweep down if he tried to drive on through to the station, now a tantalizing mile or two ahead. Another butte stood off to the right, and he pointed and shouted.

"Over there, boys! And it's going to be a fight for our lives!"

Scarcely needing to be told that, the men scattered and went driving for the knoll, not the best place for a defense but the only one they could hope to reach. The whoops of the Indians rolled after them, and the war party came off the hill in a wide wave. The volunteers didn't know it yet, but they had run into White Bird, heading out on the southern trail to the Clearwater Valley as ordered by Joseph.

The separating distance was so narrow that, well before the volunteers reached the knoll, they were mixing with the fastest Nez Percé horsemen. Unable to bring their rifles into play at such close quarters, they used their revolvers, and once or twice somebody had to club a rifle and beat off an Indian to keep from being pulled from the saddle. In this chase Frank Vansise's horse was killed, but Johnson managed to take the thrown rider up behind him.

Wilmot found himself on slightly higher ground than Randall, Cearley, Bartlett, Fenn, Evans, and the double-riding Johnson and Vansise, who streaked along the depression below him, with the others lost somewhere in the dust. He saw Randall's horse go down, spilling the rider; Wilmot jumped from the saddle and began shooting, and managed to drive back the crowding Indians. His bristling stand let the others get their rifles in action, and they included some of the best shots in Idaho. Momentarily the Indian assault was stopped.

Randall lay by his dead horse, gravely wounded, and Houser rode in wounded in the breast, and Ben Evans had been killed. Wilmot gave Randall water, but he threw it up

and died, and the survivors formed in a line where they
scooped out breastworks and managed to hold back the
howling Indians who soon swept in again.

The fighting was close enough to be heard and seen at the
Cottonwood station, and if they could hold out long enough
they figured they would have help from there. But their
ammunition wouldn't last forever, and pretty soon the Indians worked around and whacked them with a wicked en-
filading fire. Time passed, and it grew apparent that no help
was coming from Perry's command. Finally Vansise offered
to try to get through to the regulars and struck out by
himself.

On the Cottonwood hill the cavalry was fully aware of
what was happening about a mile and a half south of them.
The pressure against them had stopped in the night, but
Sergeant Simpson had some troops throwing up additional
entrenchments on the south side of the hill. From that position he saw the Indians swoop down on something coming
along the Mount Idaho road and made a pretty shrewd guess
as to what it was. Word was rushed to Captain Perry, whose
binoculars appraised him more fully of the situation. Officers
and men rushed to get ready to pile into it, but their commanding officer stopped them cold.

"As you were," Perry said curtly. "We couldn't get there
in time to save them."

The officers looked at him in astonishment, and the men
widened their eyes. It was plain those were volunteers coming in response to the call for help. That little force had
undertaken it and crossed miles of dangerous prairie, and
here were 150 trained soldiers without an enemy around
them declining to go a couple of miles because there were
enemies with guns over there.

Perry had taken his lumps in Lahmotta Canyon, and they

had twisted him. Diffidence had marked everything he did since, and he still suffered from bad scouting, believing the hostiles to have twice their actual number of fighters. When he saw the Nez Percés separate and pull out, that morning, he had only felt relief where once he might have seen a chance to end the war quickly. Now he saw no way the handful of volunteers could be rescued before they were wiped out. Forty-six men of his command had already been lost at Lahmotta and on the prairie, and he had to consider that, if he weakened the guard on the supply train, another band might swoop in and take it. Rationalization though this was, it set him stubbornly in his decision.

The troopers muttered and returned to their digging while the officers forced down their humane impulses and tried to keep their mouths shut. There was another stir of rebellion, however, when Vansise rode in and called for help. Two civilians, Shearer and Guiterman, turned their backs on Perry's protests and rode back with the plucky Vansise. They got through unhurt, although Shearer's horse was shot from under him just as he reached the volunteers' line. Still Perry stayed put.

Most of the Indians had swung around to the east side of the knoll occupied by the volunteers, and the fire was short range and hot. One by one the watching officers asked Perry's permission to take out a relief column, and they were all refused. Presently Sergeant Simpson, who had returned to the trenching detail, could stand it no longer and threw down his shovel. He strode back to the main command, his men following.

"By God," he announced to all within hearing, "if we don't have the officers to take us out, I'll take you out myself! Come on!"

Perry stared in astonishment, but before he could order

the man arrested half the cheering command went racing toward the picket line. Insubordination was wholesale mutiny already, and he was helpless.

Turning to Stephen Whipple, he said stiffly, "Take them out, Captain, but only to bring in the volunteers."

Whipple's command swooped off the hill and drummed the prairie as it flowed forward, and the Indians had to pull back from their positions around the volunteers. The regulars split on the knoll, swept around it, and drove the hostiles off still farther. The shouting volunteers poured in their own fire, and cavalry dust rolled up the sky as the Indians broke off completely and disappeared.

Not a man had been lost in the effort Perry believed would be ruinous.

The fighting had started at noon, and it was after four o'clock when the dead, wounded, and survivors were brought into the Cottonwood hill. The surgeon took care of the wounded, and about an hour later Bill Hunter's citizen soldiers reached the end of their hard ride from Salmon River. The situation was in hand, and the Nez Percés slid off to the Clearwater Valley. Perry placed Sergeant Simpson under arrest.

CHAPTER SIX
COLLISION AT CLEARWATER

One by one the stories had gone on the news wires, of the
rout at Lahmotta Creek, the massacre of Rains' command,
the mauling taken by the civilian volunteers, and all at once
national attention was centered on Joseph and his tiny but
valiant band. Howard's demonstration of who was boss in
the Indian country was working backward. From a distance,
and if one had no stake in the matter, this was amusing.
Close up and in high Army and Indian Bureau circles it
was downright appalling.

In Washington William Tecumseh Sherman, Commanding
General of the Army, remembered uneasily that he had as-
signed a mere nine thousand troops to hold down the whole
simmering Northwest, which this Joseph was bringing to a
boil with his successes. Sherman ordered General Wheaton's
Second Infantry out of its posts in Georgia and got it on
trains and moving west. He sent orders crackling down to
Hancock, of the Atlantic, and Sheridan, of the Missouri divi-
sions, to contribute even more troops if called for.

At Pacific Division Headquarters, in San Francisco, General McDowell was doing all he could to retrieve the situation and soon had substantial reinforcements of his own
converging on central Idaho. Three more companies of the
Fourth Artillery had been dispatched from the local presidio,
one by way of Fort Boise and the others by water. Major
Green finally got his three cavalry troops moving out of Fort
Boise on the maneuver Joseph had long since made obsolete.

Detachments of the Eighth and Twelfth Infantries were heading north from distant Fort Yuma.

The Indian Bureau was experiencing an agitation of its own. Superintendents and reservation agents grew unwontedly solicitous of their charges and promised a whole slough of improvements that had long been procrastinated. Chiefs were visited and beguiled and urged to pay no attention to what was going on in Idaho. Chief Moses found himself the special object of attention. Although he denied he was serving as a focal point for warriors off the Colville and Umatilla reservations, they were obviously in evidence in great numbers along Crab Creek. He admitted finally that he had called them to him but only to keep them under close supervision and out of trouble during the unrest. This failed to restore confidence.

But the epicenter of this growing hurricane was still over central Idaho.

Bill Hunter's hard-bitten volunteers rode escort on the casualties from the latest Cottonwood fight, taking them to Mount Idaho and burying them. Then they returned to Grangeville, where Captain Perry's command had come up with the fought-over supply train. They waited there while Howard completed a forced march from the Salmon Valley on July the ninth, his men having gone hungry all the way. The over-all command was gathered in full force for the first time, over six hundred strong. Rations and ammunition were issued from the new stores, equipment was checked, the companies mustered. The officers were briefed, and the next day this powerful expedition struck eastward in dead earnest.

The column that snaked down the falling sagebrush plateau toward the Clearwater Valley made the most impressive military demonstration ever seen in the Far Northwest; cavalry and caissons and pack train, infantry, light artillery marching as foot, over a hundred civilian volunteers, and a contingent of friendly Indian scouts.

In late afternoon Ed McConville and eighty-five men were ordered to the left to post themselves at a point north-west of Joseph's village and cut off a retreat up the canyon or down the valley of the river. McConville spanked away with the volunteers, who included the survivors from Randall's command, and Howard's command curved south on a longer march that brought it in on the east side of the Clearwater. The general designed this maneuver to hold Joseph still, so he could be subjected to proper battle.

McConville crossed Cottonwood Canyon well west of Joseph's new village and angled off down the plateau on a northward slant, careful not to warn the Indians, and he reached his objective in early afternoon. Discovering an open, grassy hill with a good view of the country he was to defend he made camp, forbade fires and placed the horses on picket. The men ate cold rations, not unhappy at being left out of the main fight to come at the village and pretty sure that few if any Indians would escape a mighty force like Howard's and manage to work down their way.

They sat around the camp, leaning against the abundant rocks, whittling and yarning. The Mount Idaho men fell to recounting the fight in which their captain was killed, and the Lewiston volunteers, a little envious, tried to top that with accounts of the fast ride they had made out of Rocky Canyon with Bill Hunter to relieve them. Arguments arose as to the need for relief, then, around three o'clock, somebody noticed Indians skulking between them and the river. They were anything but in flight from Howard, who had not had time to flush them, and there seemed to be quite a few of them.

"We're in trouble, boys," Lew Wilmot said dismally. He
was on the dour side naturally, for he had already been in
one close scrape and had left a wife and four young daughters at home. "We better dig in fast."

McConville had a look and agreed that hostilities seemed
imminent and again on the hostiles' terms.. The hill abounded
in rocks, and he ordered the men to build rifle pits by heap-
ing them in mounds about fifty feet apart, the stretched line
thus formed arcing across the face of the hill toward the
river.

Not satisfied with that, the volunteer captain called Wilmot aside. "Lew," he said worriedly, "there's no telling
where Howard is right now except we know he's somewhere
up the river. You better locate and warn him they've caught
onto us. Ask for some cavalry down here right away. We
might have the whole caboodle on our own hands."

Wilmot tightened his lips and his cinch and rode out
grimly on what would be a ride of fifteen or twenty miles
through hostile country. The men used their cups and knives
to throw dirt onto their breastworks, and the sun slid down
the sky without an attack. The men had no hope they would
be spared and were already cut off from water, with rations
sufficient to carry them only a short time. But they would
get a breather, probably, for the Indians did not care to
fight at night, dreading evil spirits, and with luck Wilmot
could get back with cavalry before another sunup. Thus
they reasoned, and the night rolled in, and about an hour
later rifles split open the spooky night the Indians were
supposed to fear.

The night was pitch black and there was nothing to shoot
at but the flash of gun flames, yet the volunteers blazed
away, well aware that it was all up to them. Fortunately, the

Indians' downhill position sent their first fire in high, creating a band of relative safety if a man could shoot over the barricades without getting too much of himself exposed above the rocks.

Bullets mowed the grass on the hill face and struck rocks and trees and screamed off into the darkness. The firing was rapid, and the Indians whooped, and the nearby horses reared and snorted and began to snap their picket ropes. That couldn't be helped for the Nez Percés had worked up on the flanks, making it suicide to try to reach the animals. A man was wounded slightly when a glancing bullet raked his arm, but that was the only casualty so far.

The Indians on the flanks began to pinch in on the rear, up the hill from the volunteers, and half the prepared entrenchments had to be abandoned while their erstwhile occupants wheeled over and tried to form a new line on the exposed side. The fire from above laid in behind the former works, but by some miracle the black hours passed with nobody else being hit.

Just before dawn the Indians broke off and went hooting up the river. The volunteers held their position until well after strong light and discovered that only fifteen of their horses remained. Some had been shot, but the bulk had fallen into Nez Percé hands. With them went the rations and extra ammunition, and the command was three-fourths afoot in the heart of Indian country.

McConville appraised the situation and said, "Howard must've jumped the village. That pulled this bunch off of us."

"And our move," a private offered, "is to get out of here while the getting's good."

That seemed sensible and, Howard's dependence on them

to break up the expected Indian rout notwithstanding, the volunteers headed back to Mount Idaho to remount and re-equip themselves.

When Ollicut came in with his war party in the early morning, with news of the attack on the citizen soldiers which had rendered them harmless, excitement buzzed through the village on the Clearwater at the mouth of Cottonwood Canyon. The Indians looked over the captured horses and examined the contents of the saddlebags, but Joseph took it as something less than cause for celebrating. Knowing the volunteers had conducted no offensives of their own, their presence on the Clearwater was warning that Howard was somewhere near with his mighty force, and Joseph called his chiefs into council.

"This sun will bring another fight," he told them, "and we must not be caught asleep. Ollicut will take his warriors back down the river to the second canyon to see that nothing gets to us from the north. White Bird will go up the Cottonwood to the west for the same purpose, and Tuhulhutsut will ride up the main river to Rabbit Creek. We must have lookouts on all the hills and be watchful for soldiers. If they come we must hold them where they are seen and protect our village."

"Let them come," White Bird said with a contemptuous twist of the mouth, "and we will destroy them."

Joseph looked at him impatiently, knowing how badly the younger man's anger distorted his vision. White Bird was brave, a capable war chief himself, but there was so much he had yet to learn. Ollicut was also confident and eager, and Tuhulhutsut, though old and weary, had his eternal, mystic fervor to fire him.

Their eyes shining, the chiefs wheeled away and rode

off with their warriors, stripped to breechclouts and moccasins and wearing armbands and war feathers. Nothing
would get past them easily, but Joseph remained disquieted.
He had considerable respect for the one-armed soldier who
now was dedicated to conquer him. Howard had to come
from the west, south, or north, where Joseph had just sent
his chiefs, yet something somewhere seemed wrong.

The morning was warm, and the village was so serene
that there seemed to be no war anywhere. He saw his wife
down by the river with some of the other young women of
the band. They were washing clothes, beating them on the
rocks, and his newborn daughter was in her *tekash,* tipped
against a rock. Above and below them youngsters were busy
at their fish traps and he saw his older daughter with them
and smiled. The old folk had found sunny spots about the
village to sit and ease their bones while they watched the
goings-on. If only, he thought, the white people would let
them live the life of their choice.

His effectiveness had been swelled by some forty warriors
when Looking Glass came out of the hills to join him at this
place, and others had slipped in to him from the subagency
at Kamiah. Looking Glass was a wise man who much preferred peace, but he would fight like a devil now that they
had given him no decent alternative. Joseph had kept him
and Yellow Bull in the village, now, to protect it if something went wrong. Or, the village being centrally located,
to send them rushing off if needed up or down the river or
in the long canyon that climbed west to the prairie.

He got his rifle and pony and splashed across the ford
and rode up on top of the east river bluffs. The flattening
country beyond was a high table, cut by canyons that fell
down to the river bottom, and eastward the terrain rolled in
receding swells to the base of the Bitterroot Mountains.

It was wooded in scattered patches, so he couldn't see far,
but the enemy could not appear from this direction without
being‚noticed by the lookouts on the western hills.

Yet Joseph remained troubled as he went back to the
village and there was cause.

Howard had crossed the command several miles up the
river and prudently continued east until he could swing
north behind a long file of hills that would hide him effectively from Indian eyes. Even as Joseph pondered the matter
the general was off there, persistently moving toward a
point where he would cut in again to the river and attack.
He had learned of McConville's plight by then, but it was
too late to send help without tipping off his own movement.
Otherwise the development was a lucky break. Joseph
would have his attention riveted on the west and could be
taken by a much greater surprise than would have been
possible otherwise.

The morning passed and noon arrived but the column
didn't halt. A few minutes after twelve Lieutenant Fletcher,
who had been off on a scout to the river, came boiling back.

"We've got them, sir," he said excitedly. "In fact we
overshot their village a couple of miles."

He went on to report what he had seen. Directly abreast
of them a fair-sized war party was on the river, apparently
watching for trouble from the direction of McConville's
volunteers. The village itself was in a canyon mouth a mile
or so upstream. On above and across from it was another
large canyon the command could use to get down to the
bottom to attack. The strategy was ready-made but the aide
was tactful enough to let the general discern it.

"Excellent," Howard said, his eyes gleaming. "This time
we've got things our way, and we'll dust their feathers."

He called up his officers and began to snap orders. Trimble's cavalry and Rodney's artillery would remain with the pack train, bring it close to the battlefield, then halt and stay with it. The other cavalry and a little artillery would rush forward to the river under Howard's personal command and open the engagement by shelling the Indians from the bluff. While artillery kept the hostiles' attention diverted, the cavalry would slip across the tableland to the descending canyon Fletcher had mentioned and tie into the village. The infantry and remaining artillery would come up on the double to support the attack. The end of the uprising was in sight, and Howard had waited long for it.

Cavalry and caissons rolled out promptly, some of them carrying the new Gatling guns that could fire shells in frightful bursts. The general pushed forward and at one o'clock had his own look at the situation down on the river, and his glasses showed it to be as described. The howitzers rolled up to the bluff without attracting attention, and the first shell went lobbing across the river to explode among the warriors down there. The Gatlings drummed away and more cannister splattered the canyon. Poised back at the head of an intervening draw, Captain Perry got the signal and took his three troops of cavalry sweeping across the table to get down to the village itself. He also had a score to settle.

It had been excellent strategy, but Fletcher hadn't discerned nor Howard taken into account the unseen factors in Joseph's dispositions. Tuhulhutsut's war party was at the mouth of Rabbit Creek, mounted and spoiling for trouble. It consisted of twenty-four warriors who instantly struck up the very canyon Perry proposed to descend for his attack. Down at the village Joseph saw through the maneuver also, and sent Looking Glass rushing after Tuhulhutsut,

while he remained with the rest of the reserve until he knew
if this shelling was a diversion for another assault from the
west.

Tuhulhutsut's braves rode like demons up the timbered
ravine, came to a transverse draw leading north and spilled
into it, quickly bursting onto the table. Off to the north they
saw the dust of horse troops boiling toward them and reacted with the intuitive fighting skill that had been with
them all the way, promptly moving into a position that
would flank the cavalry charge. Meanwhile Looking Glass,
following the skirmishers, took his own men on to where
the main canyon headed, thus fronting the cavalry when it
swept in. In minutes the first mounted fight of the war was
on at a furious pace.

Perry still suffered the hostility of his command, although
he had temporarily released Sergeant Simpson from arrest
because he was needed on the march. The men themselves
were galled by the record they had made, by the terrific
losses they had suffered, and here was a chance to redeem
all that. This was true cavalry fighting, yet it was different
too. All about them in the swirling dust nearly naked Indians
rode and whooped in full view with seemingly charmed
lives. They used their hips for gun mounts or swung down
to shoot under the necks of their ponies. They had a nerve-
racking taste for pulling a man from the saddle to finish
the fight with a knife on the ground.

Guns yapped and snarled, and bullets burned through
the smoky dust, and hoofs and shots rolled into a roar that
swept up to the distant mountains. Men fell from the saddle,
horses collided in the blinding dust, and sometimes a
fractious mount carried its rider clear out of the battle.
There was less disorder than the participants realized, and
to the watching general it meant one particular thing. As

had always happened so far, he was going to fight this one according to the Indians' plan, not his own.

The warriors had bought time for reinforcements to get behind them, then they pulled back into the timber. The cavalry had served the army force in the same way, and the infantry and artillery came up in the rear as quickly as they could get there. Soon the horse troops dismounted and formed a skirmish line to hold onto what they had neither wanted nor expected to fight for, a piece of sage-covered tableland still a mile away from the village.

Howard moved onto the battlefield and set up a command post on the east edge of the big canyon-bound plateau before him. The ground slanted off in a series of falls toward the river, and over to the right a second canyon marked the northern limit of the field. The supply train had come on and stopped about a mile farther north, but Howard at the moment was too busy to worry about it. As the foot battalions ran up he strung them along the bluff of the main canyon, which the Indians defended, and across the table along a transverse draw that depressed the slope somewhat short of the river. There were a few Indians on the flat beyond that draw, and if they got there in force they could enfilade his whole line.

Down on the river Joseph had decided that he had already met the main attack. He called in White Bird and Ollicut from their outposts and sent Ollicut up the north canyon to the table to present Howard with a brand new front. White Bird went up the south and main canyon with instructions to get on the flat between the transverse draw and the river bluff, a possibility Howard had already worried about. Then Joseph went up to the battlefield himself, an untutored war chief pitting himself against a West Point graduate.

Howard was doing his best now that he had a stabilized battlefield in open country. The only results he saw were the walking wounded emerging from the dust, and men more grievously hurt being carried in by comrades, and he knew that somewhere out in the turmoil many others lay dead in the mounting heat. The surgeons set up a medical station that soon became a hospital in a clump of trees on a high spot in the center of the field, and Howard moved his command post down near to it.

He had barely made this change when Indians appeared along the north canyon in numbers, as he had feared they would, and he had to pull infantry out of the west line and send it over there. That was barely accomplished when more Indians worked out on the slope across the transverse draw, where he had also feared to see them, and he had to thin the south line and send two companies scurrying down there to replace the ones he had just withdrawn. The result was a front nearly two and a half miles long, dangerously gapped, and fortified only by the rifle pits the men could throw up with trowel bayonets. Finally he learned that he had lost a spring at the head of the north canyon on which he had depended. It was their only source of water, now that they were cut off from the river.

Presently the Indians beyond the draw shoved sharpshooters out in front of them, and other expert shots glued themselves to high points beyond the two side canyons. Before anything could be done about that the hostiles along the south bluff came forward in a howling charge. It was furious, every gun on either side turning hot in its user's hands.

The regulars took it, held a few minutes, then had to give ground. This forced the commanders on the resulting salients to fall back to straighten the line. Thus the tide of battle turned against Howard, which was hastened when a new attack poured in from the north bluffs. During this the Indians beyond the draw delivered a blistering crossfire that forced the whole line to contract. Before long it formed a horseshoe around the hospital, command post, and mounts, and the single advantage was that this tightened the line until it again could hold ground.

Howard turned to an aide and said crisply, "Wilkinson, it doesn't appear that we'll have this settled by dark. Tell Trimble and Rodney to get the train in before these devils cut us off on all sides."

The lieutenant galloped away, and the sun slid down the sky, and just before dark the train circled in under its heavy guard and pulled inside the lines.

A long and painful night was to follow. The men had breathed dust and powder smoke through a blistering afternoon, their canteens were empty, and thirst raked their burning throats like spurs. Yet their discomfort was nothing to the suffering of the wounded, in whom shock and blood loss had induced a terrible need for water. Men offered to attempt to circle the deadly canyons and get down to the river with canteens, but before they could start Indian skirmishers moved in on the east, their last open flank.

So they chewed hardtack and tried to swallow it and lay in their rifle pits with their eyes aching from fatigue and from the effort to see into the lethal blackness. But the Indian fire dwindled to scattered shots and, from somewhere, coyote cries began to rip up the strange, ensuing silence. Thirsty horses and mules pulled on their pickets, and company officers passed along the lines, encouraging their men.

Howard himself made the rounds, complimenting and thanking them. There was something about a general officer that could enhearten an enlisted man anytime, and this helped. Yet in the small hours too many of them remembered that their situation was strangely like Reno's, a year ago, besieged on the hill above the Little Big Horn, and this was hard to keep out of their minds.

At nightfall Joseph had gone down to the river with half his warriors, not knowing if McConville would work upstream afoot, in the night, and attack his undefended village. The old men were eager for news and generous in their praise, which he turned aside. He knew the strength had not been drained from the great force confronting him, a force four times his own this time. He went to his lodge for a handful of dried beef, and his heart grew big when his wife cried out in relief at his safety.

"How goes it?" she said, hurrying to him. "Will you drive them away again?"

He slanted his smile down to her through the smoky firelight. "If the fox can drive away the buffalo."

"Then will they let us alone?"

He shook his head. "Never in this country, but there are others. Beyond the mountains and beyond the prairies, maybe we would be allowed to live our own lives."

Dawn split along the ridge of the Bitterroots, the command stirred to what would be another intensely hot day, and bullets sledged in from the Indians to confirm that they were still on all sides. Dry hardtack would not go down, there could be no coffee or even a drop of moisture for the parched throats of the wounded. Howard knew that the lost springs had to be retaken at any cost.

They were a little east of the end of the Nez Percés who occupied the north canyon bluff, but sharpshooters had got in the rocks and trees around the springs, and the spot was within range of the Indians' main line along the canyon. So Howard ordered his own fire stepped up until the scattered shooting became a din, and the howitzers threw shells into the lower canyon, then thirst-crazed troops charged all along the north line. This diversion let a picked platoon sweep over the springs and drive out the sharpshooters, and the line managed to hold its new position.

Water soon came inside the lines in canteens and camp kettles. The wounded were relieved, the men quenched their thirst, and there was eventually enough to dole out a little to the mounts and pack mules. Howard ordered the cavalry to drive the Indians off the east flank, and they did so although it took the rest of that morning. Shortly after noon he turned the lines over to Miles and Perry and drew out Miller's artillery battalion on which to concentrate his own attention.

Captain Marcus Miller was cool and ready and said he could deliver what Howard wanted. Howitzers were wheeled into place, and foot squads slipped down the slope with Gatling guns, and all at once a shelling such as the field had not yet seen was focused on the south and main canyon. It lasted for about ten minutes and when it stopped Miller's whole battalion went charging along the canyon bluff and mixed it hand to hand with the Indians.

The shouting command poured it on along the other fronts and the Indians broke apart. They fought stubbornly, but retreated out of the south canyon, and the companies on the west drove their opponents straight down the river bluff to the bottom. After that there was no use for the Indians to try to hold the north canyon, and these withdrew to the river.

Caissons and Gatlings rushed down to the river bluff for the windup and shelled what soon proved to be an empty village. During the night Joseph had given orders for his people to pack up and be ready to leave when he gave the command.

CHAPTER SEVEN

THE MARCHING MERRY-GO-ROUND

The dust was gone, and along the edge of the woods long delayed cookfires sent pleasant little jets of smoke into the broiling heat of the afternoon. The men fried quantities of bacon and boiled gallons of coffee, but there was no celebrating. The surgeons had reported twenty-four wounded, one of whom was Sergeant Simpson, officially a prisoner. Thirteen dead had been gathered off the field and buried in a common grave. In late afternoon the field was cleared of its littered rifles, bayonets, cartridge boxes, canteens, haversacks, and meat-ration cans. Then the command marched down the canyon it had expected to thread twenty-four hours earlier and bivouacked on the Clearwater by the deserted Indian lodges.

The men bathed in the river and ransacked the lodges for plunder, and the officers removed their own patinas of sweat and dust at a distance upstream. After a swim Captain Stephen Whipple sat on the bank smoking a pipe with his old friend from the Wallowa cantonment, First Lieutenant William Winters.

"Well, the general's calling it a victory, Bill," Whipple said. "What do you think?"

"That we can't stand to win many more like it," Winters replied. "And I think something else. For once we had our kind of field with a three-to-one edge at least, and still they darned near walked over us. What does that prove?"

"That we're up against a mighty capable bunch of Indians with a genius for a leader. Everything about that fight was for the book—the dispositions, the maneuvers, and the withdrawal before they were seriously hurt."

"You're talking treason," Winters said and grinned.

"I'm talking facts. The Army's alibied itself for years with the excuse that Indian fighting's in a class by itself. When they can kick us around in our kind of fight, it makes a man think. It was the howitzers and Gatlings that beat them. If we hadn't had them we might well have been wiped out."

"I wonder where they'll go from here?"

"They went down the river toward the Lolo Trail, and you know what that suggests.

"Montana. I hope we don't have to chase them that far."

"The east side of the Bitterroots," Whipple said, "is in the Dakota Department and not our worry. To be honest, I hope the Indians make it there."

"Still worrying about manifest destiny?"

Whipple wrinkled his brow. "Well, it bothers me. We pride ourselves on being a nation of rugged individualists. We're supposed to love freedom, and we welcome the oppressed of Europe by the hundreds of thousands and put no restrictions on where they're going to live or how. Yet we've been trying our damnedest to destroy a little handful of aboriginals who ask nothing more than that same freedom. We're not dirty bastards, either; we really think we've got to do it. That doesn't make much sense."

"The Army's a poor place for a philosopher."

"Maybe. But it's not the Army that wants to do this. It's the people and their government."

"Just the same the Army gets the dirty work." Winters knocked the dottle from his pipe. "And it's not doing it so good, either. If the general wanted to wind this thing up, we'd be on the Nez Percés' heels right now and we'd hound them till they're worn out. It's the only way to beat them."

"He doesn't operate that way. He'll dissipate what advantage he gained here and have to start from scratch."

Winters nodded. "Like a prizefight. Go a round and rest, go another and rest again. Want to bet on how many rounds this fight goes?"

"No, thanks."

After a night's sleep the wounded men were dispatched for Fort Lapwai under cavalry escort, and the balance of the command headed north down the valley in the direction the Nez Percés had fled. Twelve miles below the battlefield was another good river crossing, near the Kamiah subagency, which was on the old buffalo hunters' trail over the Bitterroots to Montana. The men said they wouldn't mind if the hostiles headed east and kept going until they reached New York City, but to Howard the prospect of their escaping into Montana was alarming. As usually happened after his leisurely periods of fussing over details, Howard again hurried the command. Not until now did it occur to him that it would be a good idea to send cavalry forward to try to head off an Indian crossing at Kamiah. He sent Perry's and Whipple's troops rushing north for that purpose.

Whatever his inner misgivings, Stephen Whipple never forgot that he was a soldier, but David Perry was the senior officer and in command of the mission. The troopers covered the distance in about two hours, and when they came to the last hill before the crossing they saw below them a scene of frantic haste at the river. The Indians were all there, and it was obvious that they had reached there the night before and made camp on the near bank while they built skin boats to get over. Now some were across, some were even then on the water, but the bulk of the band was still on the near side and a ready-made target for the cavalry.

Perry shouted, "At the gallop!" and the command drummed down the hill, coming in under a bluff that flanked the river on the far side and into a storm of bullets. A trooper went out of the saddle, the rest were thrown into confusion, and the charge ended in a dash for cover. The Indians hooted and kept shooting, and the troopers responded from their handicapped position and watched the last of the Indians get safely over the water. The Indian flankers on the bluff across from them let out one last derisive howl and pulled off.

Perry was whipped spiritually more than actually, and he waited where he was until the main column caught up. By then the Nez Percés had gone into camp openly on the other side of the river, but their warriors formed a bristling line across its front and well out on either side. Howard took a look and pulled the command back out of range and searched his mind for a military maneuver. It would have to work a miracle. The Indians had nothing but the mountains and Montana behind them and a formidable river before them that the command could not cross without being shot to tatters.

Ed McConville arrived just then with his re-equipped volunteers, and they were men who knew the country. McConville explained the lay of the land, informing the general that another trail started a few miles down the river and cut back on the east side to the Lolo Trail at a point well above the Indians' position. That offered an opportunity for Howard's favorite device of getting on two sides of the enemy and required only that he do it with sufficient secrecy to keep them in ignorance of his intentions.

He considered it worth a try and divided the command and took half of it on a feint to the south, after which it circled back toward the lower crossing. He had scarcely

covered six miles when a courier caught up to say it was no
use. The Indians had seen through it promptly and broken
camp and moved up the trail. Long before he could get
there, they would have passed beyond the point where he
had hoped to intercept them.

Frustration seemed to be something Howard accepted
patiently as part of his Christian burden, and he set the
command down at the crossing while he pondered. A kind
of inertia had seeped through them all by then, for they were
very tired from a three weeks' march that had brought
them back, on a counterclockwise circle, to a point only
fifty miles up the river from their starting point at Fort
Lapwai.

Fifty-seven men had now been killed, with seventy-one
wounded, and it was pretty obvious that they had inflicted
no such damage on the fugitive Indians. They had fought
major battles at Lahmotta and Clearwater, ferried and re-
ferried rivers, climbed up mountains and down again, and
crossed baking prairies. They had slept tentless in thundering rains and gone for long periods without food and sleep.
Their footgear was shot, their uniforms ragged and filthy,
and hardtack, bacon, and coffee was a deadly diet.

But these very hardships had gone far to make seasoned
campaigners of them. They had learned to take care of their
equipment, to respect their foe, to keep alert, and not flirt
with trouble but to meet it dead on when it came. They
liked to bitch, as soldiers have since the first armies fought
the first war, but when orders came they obeyed them and
did their best.

Despite the Indian withdrawal from the Clearwater in
good order and condition, Howard and a few officers stubbornly regarded it as some vague kind of moral victory. The
general wrote his reports in that vein and dispatched them

to Fort Lapwai for relay to the Pacific Division. An infantry captain wrote a letter to his eastern sisters saying that the badly whipped Indians were scattered and flying, that some were coming in to surrender.

There was a flimsy basis for that last claim. On the second day of the command's sojourn at Kamiah, a band of treaty-Indian buffalo hunters under Red Heart came down the mountain trail to return to the reservation. Since they came into the crossing peacefully they were taken for surrendering hostiles despite their protests and were made prisoners and sent off to Fort Vancouver, down the Columbia, to be held.

This set Howard in the conviction that he was breaking the fighting spirit of the hostiles, and he decided to crack it a little more. Major Edwin C. Mason was dispatched up the trail with some cavalry, McConville's mounted volunteers, and a few treaty-Indian scouts. They had orders to overtake the fugitives, then two marches from the crossing, and heckle them.

The detachment followed the trail up through the yellow pine into the tangled mountains. They couldn't have got off it if they tried, for it was littered, and now and then a horse was found, worn out by the forced marching and either dead or abandoned. They came, on the second day, to Mussel Creek where the Nez Percé scouts, in the lead, ran into an ambush. One was killed, another wounded, and three suffered the ignominy of having their weapons taken away from them. This suggested that the fugitives were not yet ready for wholesale surrender, and Mason took the command back down the trail to the crossing.

Howard received dispatches from his superiors and fired off more of his own, and the big command remained immobilized where it was for several days more. The men didn't understand why, but it was a welcome change. Supplies and, which was even better, the piled-up mail came over from Fort Lapwai. And somebody discovered a camp of reservation Indians not far away where chickens could be bought, along with eggs, milk, and vegetables.

Finally Howard got going and, a week after their arrival at the crossing, three companies were left to hold the west end of the Montana trail. The rest of the command swung back to Fort Lapwai to learn that a great deal had gone on there in their absence. Supplies were piled all over the fort but, more important, the regiment of Second Infantry had finished its long run from Georgia, and three more cavalry troops had arrived from Fort Boise.

Again maps were available, and Howard and his staff poured over them, paying particular attention to a relief map of the Northwest that showed the nature of their problem. This section of Idaho was part of the Columbia basin and, slashing down from Canada, various ranges of the Rockies separated it from the plains of eastern Montana. The western part of Montana was a mixture of mountains and interlocking valleys, the northernmost being drained by Clark Fork of the Columbia. A military and freight road had long since been constructed along this fork to connect the Columbia River ports with the Montana mining camps.

"Excellent," the general said after a long study, and his aides knew he had conceived his strategy.

Lieutenant Fletcher said, "Yes, sir?"

Howard drew a finger along the blue line of Clark Fork. "We must have two columns, one to follow this route to Camp Missoula which, as you know, sits at the foot of the Bitterroot Valley where the Indian trail comes down from the mountains. What do you think of that?"

"Ah," Fletcher said dubiously, "the hammer and anvil idea again, sir?"

"Exactly. The trick is not to hurry the hostiles, so the northern column can get in place at the east end of the mountain trail ahead of them. Then the second column will move east by way of the trail and Joseph will be driven down to his destruction. He can't shuttle sidewise again, not in those mountains."

"But what if he beats the Clark Fork column, sir?"

"The Montana forces must be alerted to prevent that, particularly Camp Missoula and Fort Shaw. Gibbon's at Shaw, you know, a splendid soldier. He knows Indians."

Again telegrams flashed over the wires, and Howard described and obtained approval for the ambitious new undertaking. A column under General Frank Wheaton, comprised of his Georgia infantry, an additional troop of cavalry from Fort Walla Walla, and a company of volunteers would strike out along the northern route that Howard had described. Howard himself would return to the Kamiah crossing with his own column, drop off the three cavalry units recently arrived from Fort Boise to act as a rear guard at the crossing, pick up the three companies he had left there and, ignoring departmental limits, strike out over the mountain himself.

The general realized that he had brought together a force all out of proportion to its present adversary, and this had been done advisedly. By passing up through the Columbia basin with his column, Wheaton would be making a demonstration of power before the Yakima and Colville Indians who still seemed to be on the fence about entering the war.

Over in Montana several thousand hostile Sioux still ran free after General Terry's expedition against them the year before, and they also needed to be shown the folly of helping Joseph, for all his temporary success. Moreover, a tremendous clamor had been raised by the citizens of Montana

who, along with a few truths, had heard and swallowed
a great many atrocity stories, and they were extremely vocal
in demanding the proper protection.

So Wheaton got his column away on the forced march
toward Clark Fork, and Howard took his own weary command back to the Kamiah crossing. They arrived there on
Saturday and the next day laid over in accordance with the
religious dictates of the general, who delivered a solemn
sermon to the treaty Indians in the nearby camp.

But the column trailed out again on Monday morning, and
since the hostiles were many miles ahead there wasn't much
to worry about. The country was beautiful, green forests
sweeping away ridge after ridge, and the mountain streams
held trout. The general's lack of hurry suited the men, although they had taken to calling him General Day-after-
Tomorrow, and it began to be whispered that he was holding
back purposely to let the Dakota Department take care of
the Indians. That also suited them perfectly.

CHAPTER EIGHT

BEYOND THE SHINING MOUNTAINS

Although it was not the good general's intention, a transfer of responsibility to the Department of Dakota was exactly what was taking place. The department was already blood-stained, having just been the theater of the campaigns against the Sioux. Three of the principals of that war were still on hand: General Alfred H. Terry, who commanded it from his headquarters in St. Paul, and Colonels Nelson A. Miles and John Gibbon who were stationed at posts in Montana.

The Territory's population was still concentrated in the western half because of the chronic Indian trouble on the eastern plains, and the western section's geography was bent over the stony ridgepole of the Rocky Mountains. The valleys west of the Rockies were small, but fertile and scenic, and had been settled early by miners, stockmen, and farmers. The eastern valleys were part of the upper Missouri basin and were roomier. The Rockies ran on a southeast line so that the plains beyond extended farthest west in the north, between the Belt mountains and the Canadian border. The northeastern settlement was thin, while in the southeast it was much heavier.

The military establishments in the Territory had been changed from time to time, as circumstances shifted, but those activated by the Nez Percé threat were Camp Missoula, west of the Rockies but east of the Bitterroots, Fort Shaw across the Rockies on the northeastern plains and commanded by Colonel Gibbon, and a cantonment far east

of the Yellowstone River where Colonel Miles was building
Fort Keogh.

On a July morning, at the mouth of Tongue River, a fiery
sun poured on the bluffs of the Yellowstone and the high
tables that wheeled away into the haze. The soldiers and
civilian mechanics laying the foundations of the new fort
streamed sweat and cursed the country. A year before it
had been in the hands of the Sioux, who had left a reminder
up on the plateau in the form of 264 men who had died
up there with Custer, and for the life of them they couldn't
see why it had been worth fighting for.

They were three hundred miles from the spicy life of the
Western towns and mining camps, were supplied only peri-
odically when steamboats came up the Yellowstone, and
they didn't even get their mail until it was stale. The
civilians could quit and depart, which they did in droves,
but the soldiers had no such choice for they were troops of
the Second and Seventh Cavalries and companies of the
Fifth Infantry, tied there by enlistment papers.

Colonel Nelson A. Miles sat in his headquarters tent that
hot morning, staring at a lengthy dispatch he had just received from departmental headquarters. After a moment he
frowned across the plank table at Colonel Samuel D. Sturgis,
who commanded the Seventh Cavalry that recently had been
Custer's pet.

"More trouble, Colonel?" Sturgis asked.

"I'm afraid so, Sam." Miles rubbed his luxuriant mustache
with a forefinger. "Howard's let the Nez Percés get away
from him."

Sturgis came forward in his chair, a stocky man with wavy
hair, an amiable round face, and a drooping mustache that
hung over his mouth to join a curly goatee. "They're crossing
into our department?"

"They're in the Bitterroots right now."

"Blazes," Sturgis said explosively, "what can we do about it? That's Gibbon's territory, four hundred miles from here."

Miles smiled. He was an erect man, slightly sharp-featured, with a strong nose separating keen eyes, and his thick hair nearly touched his shoulders because of a short neck. He had arrived at the mouth of the Tongue the previous August with orders to straighten out the fiasco created by Custer's defeat. In October he had met and beaten Sitting Bull at Cedar Creek, driving the chief into Canada. In January he whipped Crazy Horse up on Tongue River. Only two months ago he had bested Lame Deer and started work on the fort that was supposed to keep them all subdued permanently.

"For one thing," Miles said, "we can keep the Sioux from pitching into it. This Joseph's an astonishing fellow. Gibbon's to try to stop him when he comes out of the mountains, but if he fails we'll have him on our hands. It's pretty obvious that they're heading for buffalo country. They've always been friendly with the Crows, who can give us enough trouble by themselves."

"Gibbon should be able to handle them," Sturgis mused. "He's a pretty rough boy."

He rose, stretched, and walked out into the heat, and Miles picked up a copy of a Virginia City newspaper, *The Madison*, that had just come down the Yellowstone by mail rider. He smiled as he read the headlines: "Missoula in Peril! The Governor Calls for Volunteers! Every Man that Can Go Wanted at Once!" Howard's performance, he mused, had depressed the Army's stock considerably.

More urgent orders had reached Fort Shaw, which was situated on Sun River twenty miles up from the Missouri and near the base of the Rockies. A year before, the fort had sent Colonel John Gibbon and the Seventh Infantry to form one of the three columns General Terry had planned to throw against the Sioux until Custer's vanity precipitated ruinous action. Now it protected the settlers of Sun Valley, and stood between the Blackfoot reservation and the settlements farther south, and kept an eye open for stray Sioux from Canada.

Gibbon was a tall, handsome man with straight dark hair and a bristling mustache and goatee. An aggressive, sometimes brutal officer, he let out a snort when he read the intelligence received from Idaho by way of San Francisco that Howard had let the Nez Percés slip through his fingers and as yet had not even started in pursuit.

Gibbon was expected to perform some kind of holding miracle while Wheaton swung around by way of Clark Fork and got into position, and Gibbon had a strong feeling that the Nez Percés were not going to co-operate in that. He had his own command scattered thinly where it was needed already, and moving enough men across the Rockies to the Bitterroot Valley would leave this whole region open to the Blackfeet and Sioux. He was exactly as far from the east end of the Lolo Trail as Howard was at that moment.

"What in hell," he yelled at the post adjutant, Lieutenant C. A. Woodruff, "am I supposed to do from here?"

The lieutenant needed informing before he could answer, and even when fully apprised of the situation he had no solution to offer.

"What's Rawn's strength at Camp Missoula?" Gibbon asked.

Woodruff riffled through a file of reports and said, "Four officers and twenty-five men."

Gibbon threw back his head and laughed. "Well, by God,

they'll have to hold the Indians until I, Wheaton, or Howard can get there."

He fired off a letter to Camp Missoula, explaining matters and telling Rawn to do the best he could with his own command and the help of civilian volunteers to keep the Nez Percés from coming out of the mountains until adequate reinforcements could be brought up. Much as he hated to do it, he called in outposts and finally had five companies ready to take the field, with the necessary stores and equipment.

His courier reached Camp Missoula several days before Gibbon was ready to leave the fort. The dispatch only confirmed what Captain Charles C. Rawn, commanding Company I of the Seventh Infantry, already knew he had to face. No one was sure how the news first reached the valleys of the Bitterroot and middle Clark Fork rivers, but it had arrived and created a near panic.

Missoula was the metropolis of northwestern Montana, with several brick blocks, a bank, and newspaper, and already settlers were flocking to it from all directions. Clark Fork wound down from the Rockies and, flowing west, was joined by the north-flowing Bitterroot near the town. Camp Missoula was just up the latter river, and a few miles farther upstream was the emergence of the threatening Indian trail from the mountains and Idaho. Once it became certain that the Nez Percés were coming, it was equally evident to the imaginative settlers that all the horrors reported from Idaho were to be visited on them.

The bad news had also reached Helena where the territorial governor had issued a proclamation calling for volunteers. There was a widespread response, all the towns forming companies, but individualists from all western

Montana chose the more direct method and grabbed rifles and hit out for the scene of expected action on their own. Presently there were around 150 of this sort in and about Missoula, town and camp. They were a pretty ragtag aggregation but, enheartened, Captain Rawn relied on them and dug in.

With the help of the volunteers, a log barricade was constructed across the east end of the Lolo Trail below the pass and heavily manned. Outposts were established, scouts sent out, and Rawn began to feel that he had a good chance to hold the line until the powerful forces now on the march could converge and take over. The volunteers were even more emboldened until some of them ventured too far up the trail and nearly got killed. This misadventure had a sobering effect on the whole volunteer contingent, whose members began to drift away. Presently Rawn realized it was mostly up to his regulars and himself.

Fortunately he had made a mistake that spared him the test.

The trail the Nez Percés had followed from the Kamiah crossing was nearly a hundred miles long, and they had not hurried since they had not been pressed. It was rugged going for a contingent so large, and it was hard to find forage for so many ponies. But they had not permitted themselves the luxury of carelessness, and thus knew about the barricade and heavy force concentrated there almost as soon as it was erected. But Rawn had not gone far enough into the mountains to make his stand, and the Nez Percés were able to slide off to the right and come down into the valley unopposed well south of the barrier.

Rawn was realistic enough to heave a sigh of relief. The Indians turned south up the valley, he had no orders to pursue them, and he took his little company back to camp.

The volunteers showed no inclination to take up the chase. Yet ahead of the Indians was a heavy population, particularly in the towns of Stevensville and Corvallis, for not all the settlers had come into Missoula for protection. This worried Rawn, but all he could do was send off a courier to connect with Gibbon and report what had happened.

Gibbon was pushing his five companies toward Missoula with all the vigor he could manage when he received word of the hostiles' escape. By his best estimate, from intelligence given him by the adjutant general of the Pacific Division, General Wheaton was still two weeks from Missoula, and General Howard about the same. So Gibbon had to go after the Indians without waiting for their support.

His knowledge of the country suggested that the Indians were heading for the Yellowstone, but that was too big a guess for him to gamble on trying to head them off instead of overtaking them from behind. He crowded the command harder and reached Camp Missoula on August the third, where he picked up Rawn's company and a contingent of volunteers under J. B. Catlin. He transferred his stores to light wagons and headed south up the Bitterroot Valley the next day, still having seven days to make up to overtake the hostiles.

To his relief he found no carnage as he moved south. Joseph had quickly struck a bargain with the settlers along the way, many of whom he knew from former passages to and from the buffalo country. He had told the settlers that as long as they did not molest his people he would not trouble them, and they had been all too willing to call it a deal. They had even furnished supplies, for which the Indians traded or paid cash, and that was remarkably short of the looting, slaughter, and rape they had been hearing about.

Gibbon heard that the Indians were taking their time, but he did not slack his own pace. He passed Stevensville and Corvallis, where Catlin's volunteers picked up recruits, and he got encouraging intelligence from H. L. Bostwick, scout and post guide at Fort Shaw, that the Nez Percés seemed unaware of a new army hot on their heels. On the afternoon of August the eighth, the command reached the head of the valley, where Bostwick came in again to report that the Indians had gone into camp just on the other side of the mountain.

This land lift was the western tip of the Anacondas, a part of the Rockies that the Continental Divide followed on a sharp swing to the west. A negotiable pass was cradled where the mountain joined the southern end of the Bitterroots, and an Indian trail that had become a very bad pioneer road threaded the pass to enter the Big Hole Valley and eastern Montana.

"They're on Ruby Creek," Bostwick reported, "and they must figure to stay awhile. Their ponies are showing ribs from the lack of grazing, and there's fine forage around their camp. Besides, they ain't been dragging teepee poles, and no redskin likes to sleep without a cover over his head. There's timber there and they'll likely cut poles."

"Any sign of a rear guard?" Gibbon asked.

"Nope. They don't know of any soldiers around except Rawn's little tag, and the settlers ain't made any trouble."

"Well, there are some other soldiers around," Gibbon said grimly, "and they'll damned soon know it. We'll go on at once."

It was harder than he had expected to get up the Divide, and the going was slow and tedious. Once over, he decided to leave his train in the care of one of his companies. That speeded things up, but later, when they had come fairly close to the Indian camp, he was obliged to leave his one howitzer and a pack mule loaded with ammunition, because of fallen timber on the trail, to be brought on after daylight.

A little short of daylight he found himself at the head of a canyon that fell down to Ruby Creek and the Indian camp. His command at that point consisted of seventeen officers, 132 men, and thirty-four citizen volunteers. This contingent started on down the trail, each man provided with ninety rounds of ammunition.

Meanwhile, General Howard was finally doing his utmost to catch up with the war that had now moved 150 miles ahead of him. On the day Gibbon learned he was on the heels of the hostiles, Howard was still on the Lolo Trail where some men came out from Missoula to inform him, for the first time, that Joseph had long since escaped into the valley. The general's unhurried advance to that point had been calculated, for Wheaton was expected to arrive in the Bitterroot Valley on the tenth, after which Howard had meant to go ramming down the trail to complete a maneuver that had been rendered obsolete nearly two weeks before.

"Well, it's not all bad," Howard decided when he had digested the news. "Gibbon's on Joseph's heels, and I'll be behind Gibbon, with Wheaton coming along behind me."

"The trouble is, Gen'ril," the newsbearer said, "there ain't anybody ahead of them Injuns."

Howard took his four troops of cavalry and went dashing forward, leaving the eight companies of infantry, seven of artillery, and the big pack train to come on behind. And up Clark Fork came General Wheaton with his infantry regiment, an additional troop of cavalry, and a big company of Walla Walla volunteers.

CHAPTER NINE

AT THE PLACE OF GROUND SQUIRRELS

Here in the southwestern section of Montana the Continental Divide grew uncertain of its proper course and, after a sweeping curve to the west, reached the Beaverhead Mountains on the border of Idaho. Along this ridge it probed uneasily to the high plateau at the headwaters of the Missouri River, vaguely defined mountains called the Centennials. Again growing puzzled, it wound uncertainly eastward along this range until, near the northwestern corner of Wyoming, it got its bearings and slid off toward the Southwest and Mexico.

This semicircle of mountains was drained by half a dozen rivers that converged at the open end to give birth to the Missouri River. One of the largest of the valleys, each divided by lesser ranges, was that of the Big Hole River. This curved in a horseshoe around the Pioneer Mountains, with the higher ranges of the Divide bordering its northern and western edges.

The nutritious wild grasses of the converging valleys had early attracted stockmen, and the placer fields had brought in hordes of gold hunters who had established the towns of Bannock and Virginia City and a handful of lesser camps. Of equal importance, a busy stage and freight road, which was the Territory's only connection with the Central Pacific, ran north and south through this section, linking Helena with the railroad at Corinne, Utah. So, while the wild beauty remained, this was a fairly well populated region whose defense against the advancing Indians depended on volunteer companies quickly raised at Bannock and Virginia City so long as the regular army remained strung out far behind the Nez Percés.

But, although the settlers ahead of them did not know it, the Indians at the moment were no threat. On August the sixth the fugitives had come down Trail Creek off the Divide to the junction with Ruby Creek. Here was a favorite campground of hunting parties, not only of their generation but of their forefathers', which they called the Place of Ground Squirrels. Ruby Creek wound lazily down the valley along the edge of the mountain to join the Big Hole River, ten miles to the east, dividing a wheeling prairie of fine forage and a grassy mountain footslope studded with scattered pine.

To the fugitive Indians, Place of Ground Squirrels was a welcome sight. Their horses were nearly exhausted, and here was fine grass. The women could cut teepee poles, which they had lacked since leaving the Clearwater, and the old and young could rest. Even Joseph felt the festive mood that came upon his people, and that first night he moved about the campfires.

"We will go to the buffalo country," he told them. "We will make meat, and when that is done we will go on to Sitting Bull in the land of the red coats. When we are there and beyond reach of the soldiers, we will send some of our chiefs back to the officers of the government to talk with them. It may be they will tell us we can return to our homes, for they will know that they cannot destroy or force us. If they will not agree to that, we will ask to be given land in Montana near the Sioux, and maybe that will be done for us."

This brought a great shouting from his people, some of them learning for the first time what the chief's plan for them had been. But others, like old Tuhulhutsut, were still suspicious and restless.

"The white people keep no promises," the medicine man intoned in the chantlike way he talked. "They never have and they never will. We must drive them from our country, as the sky spirit has told us."

"Enough, old chief," Joseph said curtly. "The war is over; we have left it behind us. We have made a truce with the settlers, and we will shoot none of them and no soldiers who do not shoot at us first, should we see them. We will take no horses and, unless our women and children grow hungry, we will take no cattle. We will do nothing that has the look of war, and the people of Montana will stay our friends."

"I trust none of them," White Bird said bitterly. "We should have warriors behind and ahead of us, just as we did on the mountain trail."

"I tell you the settlers have agreed to peace," Joseph insisted. "They are not like the settlers of Idaho. We will do nothing that shows distrust and fear."

The old men saw the wisdom and largeness of his view and agreed with him, and the camp grew merry. The first night was spent without shelter, but the next day the women cut lodge poles and raised a village, for the first time since the Clearwater, on the east bank of Ruby Creek. The men herded the ponies, placing part of the big herd down the creek and the rest across the stream on the gentle footslope of the mountain. There were fish in both streams, which drew the children, and the old ones found many a place to sit, smoke, and soak up the Montana sun.

The village, when erected, ran for about an eighth of a mile in two rows of teepees. The lodges of Joseph and Ollicut were on the south and upstream end and were the

closest to the creek, while those of White Bird and Tuhulhutsut were on the lower end. That night there was more
laughter, singing, and dancing, for the war was behind them,
and they were fair on the way to the buffalo country. Then
slowly the campfires died and they vanished into their teepees and had no way of knowing that the talking wires had
been busy throughout the Northwest and there was no
peace for them anywhere.

At that same hour Colonel Gibbon's force of 182 men had
left its horses and proceeded on into the Trail Creek canyon
on foot. It came to a place where the sounds of the Indian
camp reached its ears, now mainly the barking of dogs and
the crying of babies, where it halted and lay down to wait for
daylight. It remained there for some two hours before the
camp grew wholly quiet. Gibbon then sent Bostwick down
on a scout.

When Bostwick returned with a reassuring report, the
big force moved on in complete silence. It passed an old
buffalo wallow as it wound onto Ruby Creek, where it
turned downstream along the flat behind the willows across
from the camp. There it took position, the volunteers upstream and the regulars below them, the line thus formed
reaching the length of the village. It then lacked about an
hour until daylight, when the attack would start.

Incredible luck, Gibbon told himself. The Indians hadn't
had out a sentry.

But an old Indian and some itchy-fingered volunteers were
to mar the perfection of his attack. The Indian was Natalekin
who had gone early to his blankets and thus awakened
before the new day was quite born. His horses were with the
herd on the mountainside and, since they were not guarded,
he was uneasy about them. Stepping from his teepee on the
upper end of the village, he splashed over the creek in the

pale starshine to see about them, and this took him within range of Catlin's Montana volunteers. He was moving straight toward them and would let out a yell of warning if he saw them, so three of the volunteers fired at him and the old man fell dead.

Gibbon, who had seen the man himself, muttered to his adjutant, "The fools! Why didn't they make him a prisoner?" but it was too late. The volunteers had themselves given the warning they had sought to prevent, and the attack had to begin at once.

Joseph was sleeping beside his wife in his teepee on the upper end of the village, the young baby beside its mother, the older daughter beyond a screen. He heard the shots across the creek and sprang to his feet, not fully awake, and an outcry rang from nearby lodges, "We are attacked! We are attacked!" He groped for his moccasins and couldn't find them, then caught up his rifle.

He stepped out into bullets coming like ice pellets blown by a blizzard. The whole reach of willows beyond the creek gave birth to them, and he recognized the dreaded chatter of Gatling guns. Wheeling back to the teepee flap, he growled, "Take the children and hide!" to his wife.

"But where?" her choked voice asked.

"Up or down the creek. The soldiers are across from the village."

He was still stunned, and it seemed that none of them could survive the bullets punching through the teepees and bringing screams from dying throats. He lifted his ringing voice in a rallying cry to the warriors, who had been as confused as he by the merciless attack. He stood fearlessly, his orders boring through the yammer of rifles and Gatlings, and he saw his people crawl away from their lodges. Now and then a warrior went stumbling by, and he saw all too many of them die on their feet.

When Looking Glass appeared out of the confusion, Joseph said, "See to the women and children! Have Yellow Bull take some old men and move the ponies!" On the heels of the old chief came Ollicut, and Joseph said to him, "When the women and children are out of the village we must scatter! See to it!"

All through the village teepees had been aroused in the manner of Joseph's. The three initial shots, before the main attack, awakened the adults and got them on their feet where many were cut down in the terrible fire that erupted from Gibbon's whole line. Half the warriors were unable to arm themselves, and their first thoughts were to get their families to safety. Some attempted to start their wives and children moving, others buried them under their blankets and robes and told them not to move. Then they ran outside, dropped flat, and began to shoot into the willows.

But before any of them could do much to stabilize a defense, the white men charged. Maintaining their murderous fire, they broke across the creek and came streaming out of the willows on the near side. The charge was directed at the upper half of the village, where in a moment soldiers and warriors were locked in a death struggle. This served to organize the other warriors, who ran up from the lower end of the village carrying, if they could not get hold of their rifles, their knives and war clubs.

The noncombatants in the lower village streamed into the willows farther down the creek, but many of them fell dead or wounded before they gained concealment. Some of the soldier fire was aimed at them deliberately, regardless of age

or sex, and some of the women had children die in their arms
as they ran. But more and more of them reached hiding
under the bank of the creek, where bullets dropped twigs
on them like rain, and now and then a dead woman or child
floated by on the crimson water.

In the upper end of the village the noncombatants who
had not escaped earlier were caught helplessly while the
fierce hand-to-hand struggle was fought out. But the soldiers
outnumbered the armed Indians there, and some of them
were left free to set fire to the teepees. Soon an unholy
yellow light flickered over the scene of carnage, and the
screams of the helpless, trapped in the burning lodges, mixed
with the roar of violence; the thickening smoke soon mantled
the whole village.

Within twenty minutes of the onslaught, the last warriors
were driven out, and the soldiers were in possession of the
camp. It was heady stuff, for they had accomplished with
one fourth the force what General Howard had failed at so
miserably. They set to with a will to finish burning the village
while the rosy streaks of dawn split the sky. The growing
light revealed some of their own among the dead Indians,
and this released a ferocity in them that they vented on
the wounded Indians they found.

"This is how to fight Injuns!" a volunteer ripped out. "And
the ones that got away won't get far once we run off their
cayuses!"

The light strengthened, and from the willows upstream
and down, and from the rocks thickly dotting the flat all
about, shots whipped into them from Indian sharpshooters
they could not locate. They were perfect targets in the
growing day, and they knew it and headed on the double
for the willow-bordered creek. The Indian fire only increased,

and some of them never got there. Then somebody started to run for it, and a rout was on.

The jeering of the Indians rolled from three sides, and the disorganized command crashed into the willows and splashed through the water. The Nez Percés had not been idle, nor had they fled. All through the fighting, more and more of the unarmed warriors had entered lodges not yet burning to find weapons, and a number had taken them from dead and wounded soldiers. Once all the noncombatants who could be saved were out of the camp, they had dispersed in accordance with orders from Joseph relayed by Ollicut early in the attack. Now they had achieved an encirclement except for the creek flank, and when the troopers panicked and fled from the village the Indians came boiling after them.

Gibbon could no nothing to restore order to the command which, once back on the mountain side of the creek, broke in two directions. Part of it headed upstream toward Trail Creek and escape on the trail to the Bitterroot Valley. The rest made directly up the slope to where, some four or five hundred yards away, stood a patch of pine on a sloping flat.

The Indians, who had seemed precious few previously, appeared to have multiplied tenfold. They came on recklessly, and half a hundred separate fights broke out along the footslope. Knives and war clubs vied with clubbed rifles, and from the willows came the screams of wounded soldiers begging not to be left behind. The troops heading for Trail Creek saw the hopelessness of flight and changed direction, hoping to make it to the timber where so many others had fled. The fight raged up the slope, and most of them got into the south end of the timber where they were able to make a stand that drove the Indians back.

Gibbon reached the timber with only his adjutant and

bugler accompanying him, and he knew the command had
got itself in a bad spot. A good many of the Indians were
mounted by then and streaming all over the vicinity. Some
of them headed for the Trail Creek Canyon, and his heart
contracted when he remembered the ammunition mule and
howitzer he had left up there to be brought on at daylight.

He issued orders for the men to conserve their remaining
cartridges, and he set them to digging rifle pits along the
edges of the timber. It was a frighteningly loose line when
he had covered all four sides, but that was imperative for
the Indians had slid into positions all around the timber.
They were only sharpshooters, but that was enough. A
soldier could hardly raise his head without drawing instant
fire that was breathtakingly accurate. He saw Indians moving off the horses on the hill above the timber, and others
were moving the herd on the flat downstream from the
smoking village.

The sun was still less than an hour high, and this was the
result of the dawn attack for which the command had waited
so eagerly. An unestimated number of dead lay in the village
and on the open slope, abandoned wounded men keeping
them company, and stragglers who had not made it to the
timber cowered in fear in whatever cover they could find.
There was no water in the timber, and they had no rations
beyond what was in their belt cans.

Gibbon huddled with the few officers he could bring together and admitted frankly that their chances were not
good. There was a slight chance that Bostwick, the scout,
could slip through to the horses after dark and make his way
back to Howard and get the general's cavalry moving up
pellmell. An effort was made to find the scout only to turn
up the information that the last man who saw him had seen
him killed. A couple of officers offered to try it, but they

all knew this was whistling in the dark. Their horses were not going to be where they had been left, even if the Indians could be kept out of the timber, by the time night came again.

Then they heard two shots from the howitzer, somewhere up the canyon, and no more. That told the story. The ammunition the troops needed so desperately had fallen into Indian hands.

Smoke daubed the sky over the village, but the men on that edge of the woods could see little else but teepee tops due to the willows along the creek. There had been about a hundred lodges, and they had managed to set fire to only part of them, so the Indians still had much of their supplies and their pony herd was still intact. They now owned the countryside and rode about at will, and pretty soon a wailing rose from the camp, indicating that the women had moved back in to discover their dead. Sometimes the voices of men rang out, unintelligible but charged with fury, and this impressed the surrounded command more than the women's weeping or the crying of babies they had heard in the dark hours before they came down from the mountain.

CHAPTER TEN

AND THEY HEARD THE SOLDIERS CRYING

The Indian advantage was now so great that it took only half the warriors to keep the soldiers pinned down in the timber, with the rest free to scour the canyon for more. Meanwhile the surviving noncombatants came out of hiding and returned to the village, which was out of rifle range and screened by the willows from the hill. This security was of little importance to many of them, for while they still lived they had had their hearts destroyed.

They had left dead and wounded up and down the creek, but what they saw in the ravaged village by light of day tore from them the first concerted outcries of grief and rage. Most of their dead were here, lying among dead soldiers, and it was not easy to see this and hear the wounded children and women crying in pain.

Illatsat, a handsome boy loved by the whole village, lay shot and dead on the rocks by the creek. A woman half-floated in the nearby water, her head on the gravel bar, with a wound in her left breast that no longer bled. A little girl wandered blindly, seeking parents who were no more, holding up a shattered arm. A young warrior, Wahlitits, lay dead under the still body of his wife. She had his rifle clutched in her hands, and the soldier who killed her husband lay dead in front of them, shot by her before she died.

In a detached teepee erected the night before for a woman in labor, the woman, midwife, and newborn baby were all found dead, the head of the baby crushed. In the burned teepees were the charred bodies of children who had been hidden there, and in one a baby lay crying on its dead mother's breast, waving an arm from which dangled the hand, held only by a shred of skin and flesh. Thus, at the Place of Ground Squirrels, the destiny of the white race had been made manifest.

Once he knew the survivors were safe, at least for the moment, Chief Joseph came off the hill and went to the village. The night horses had all been killed in the first attack, and one of his main concerns had been to save the main herd, without which his people would be trapped and helpless. He had himself gone onto the hill in his bare feet to drive that band of ponies to safety. He rode into the desolate camp now, just as a party of warriors came in with a white man they had captured in the willows up on Trail Creek, a volunteer who had been cut off from the command.

A cry of "Kill him!" rose from the watchers, but Joseph held up a commanding hand.

"No. I will talk to him." He knew this citizen soldier, Campbell Mitchell, who lived in the town of Corvallis in the Bitterroot Valley, and he regarded the badly frightened man with bitter eyes. "So this is how you keep the peace we made with you, and I have seen many of your kind here this morning. While we were among you, and you thought yourselves in danger, you wanted to be our friends. When we passed beyond you, and you thought yourselves safe, your hearts grew hot for war against us. I told my people we could trust you. Only that let you take us by surprise."

The settler shifted his feet and stared at the ground. The watching warriors and women pressed close to him, and he did not like what their faces showed. He raised his eyes to Joseph.

Defiantly he said, "Look! You've got things your way right

now, but if I was you I wouldn't get high and mighty.
General Howard's only a few hours away and coming fast,
and there's a volunteer company heading this way from
Virginia City on the double."

Joseph eyed him keenly. The man could be telling the
truth or lying in hope of saving his life. But before he could
speak a woman who had lost her children and brother that
morning moved forward and slapped Mitchell's face. The
volunteer gave her a vicious kick and it was over, for a
warrior shot him dead.

Joseph walked away, considering what Mitchell had said.
He dared not ignore the possibility that the settler had
spoken the truth. The war chief's own blood was on fire, now
that he knew the people of Montana were no more to be
trusted than the people of Idaho, and he yearned to destroy
the trapped soldiers on the hill. Yet he dared not expose the
noncombatants to what could be converging upon them from
the north and east, so they would have to be removed.

He called the old chiefs to him and told them to bury
the dead and prepare to move the camp. Then he returned
to the battlefield. There was little action at the timber just
then, for the soldiers were saving their shells and the Indian
sharpshooters shot only when they had a target. Yet the
warriors were not having it all their own way, and some had
died up here also. He came upon Yellow Bull to learn that
the Salmon chief's son had just been killed by a shot from
the timber.

Meanwhile White Bird and a few warriors had gone up
the Trail Creek Canyon in fear of reinforcements coming
from that direction to help the soldiers. At some distance
up the gulch they came upon a big cannon mounted on
wagon wheels and drawn by four mules. Behind came
another mule carrying packs. About eight men accompanied

the procession, two of them not wearing uniforms. The soldiers saw their peril and managed to wheel the big gun around and get off two thunderous shots that went ripping down the gulch. Then the Indians were too close to them, and two of the soldiers went legging it for the brush. The others put up a fight until one was killed and two more wounded, when the rest all went crashing into the brush to get away.

The Indians seized their prize in chattering excitement which turned into yells when the mule packs were found to contain an enormous quantity of ammunition that would fit the uncounted rifles they had picked up on previous battlefields. In their elation they did not chase the soldiers and two civilians who were hurrying off through the timber.

White Bird sent some of the braves back to camp with the ammunition while the rest removed the wheels of the canon they did not know how to use and rolled them into the brush and hid them. The party rode on to the timber at the head of the canyon and, while they did not know it, might have come upon the supply train had they gone a little farther. White Bird left sentries in the timber at the head of the canyon and returned to the battlefield.

Noon came, and a fiery sun stood over the southward mountains. By then the soldiers had been driven back from their entrenchments at the edge of the timber, squeezed in a tightening compress of rifle fire. They used their trowel bayonets to throw up new barricades, behind which they flattened themselves in a state of near helplessness imposed by the shortage of ammunition. They chewed a little hard-tack and their canteens went dry one by one, after which there would be no more water. They could hear their wounded cry for help in delirious heedlessness, down along the slope and in the willows by the creek. Now there were more dead and wounded around them in the timber. When the hostiles got into the edge of the woods, finally, they remained upright, flitting from tree to tree, co-ordinating their actions so that if a soldier raised up to fire at one Indian another shot at him with an accuracy that was unnerving.

In the village the women struck the lodges that remained undamaged and began to prepare travois from the poles and skins to carry the wounded. The dead had been gathered and buried, the wounded given the best care possible, and the chiefs consulted over the problem that now confronted them. Once the village and horse herd moved out on the trail they could be seen from the timber. They must press on into the Big Hole Valley, where the citizens might strike at them, and Howard might well come over the Divide on their rear. Both possibilities had to be guarded against, and Joseph preferred not to let Gibbon see in which direction he sent his families. In the slashing way his mind usually worked, he conceived a stratagem.

Thus in midafternoon the trapped command smelled smoke, then they saw it boil upwind from them in the thick dry grass at the edge of the timber. A cry of alarm swept down the long line, but when men raised their heads to take a look bullets crashed in from the sharpshooters. Gibbon saw in grim apprehension that they would be driven into the open in a matter of minutes to be shot down as they emerged.

He shoved to his feet, and a bullet drilled into his thigh and knocked him headlong. He gasped to a nearby officer, "They can't see through the smoke—our best chance is to fight back the fire!"

Smoke already reeked through the timber and into sensitive eyes and lungs like acid sprayed on the wind. The men coughed and choked and, half blinded by tears, those fronting the approaching flames rushed forward boldly and tried to fight back the new menace with their shirts and stamping feet. The howling Indians riddled the timber with bullets, but now they shot blindly, and the flames crept across the grass, hungrily straining toward the timber.

Embers landed in the woods and started little fires in the tinder-dry needles, but somebody always saw them in time to beat them out. Nearly blinded and coughing constantly, the command fought both enemies, and the crisscrossing bullets of both sides found an occasional blind target. This went on for what seemed hours, then the wind changed and turned the flames off to the side.

In those moments of wild confusion Joseph had achieved what he wanted. The noncombatants were quickly on the march down the valley of Ruby Creek, hidden by the smoke that rolled up the mountain behind them. He sent the old chiefs with the families and a handful of warriors to protect them. He accompanied them personally until they were well away from immediate danger, then he returned to the fight.

The fire had died out and the smoke cleared away and the fierce August sun slid on down the sky. When evening came the chief divided his warriors, taking part to join the families and to protect their camp through the night. He left the rest as a rear guard under Ollicut, who stepped up the firing into the timber and kept the soldiers ignorant that the force against them had been reduced.

The command did little return shooting, for its ammunition was all but gone, finally, and what remained had to be conserved for the charge they fully expected to come from the Indians. For those still unhurt it was tough enough to be there hungry and thirsty in the cold mountain night and hear bullets whine past them without shooting back. Some

of them became unnerved as the night progressed and began
to whimper until voices out of the darkness told them to
shut up.

Gibbon lay in his rifle pit, weakened and punished by his
wound, and regretted that he had not sent off a dispatch
to Howard, before advancing on the Indian village, and
arranged for cavalry to hurry up to him. His motive had not
been the vanity that led Custer to his doom, but the outcome seemed likely to be the same.

The Indian fire began to slack off at last, and Gibbon
deemed it prudent, at last, to try to send a detail out after
water. Volunteers offered to undertake it, and presently
they moved out, three men carrying all the canteens they
could manage quietly and the others acting as a firing party.
They crawled out of the timber without setting off a new
spasm of gunfire, and began to slither through the rocks and
sagebrush that all day had concealed the Indian sharpshooters. Foot by slow foot they wormed their way down to
the creek, having to crawl nearly a quarter of a mile.

None of them had ever felt an elation like that which
charged them when at last they could touch their lips to
water. Later they filled the canteens, and then they had the
long, lethal slope to cross again. So far they had drawn no
fire, and some of them wondered if the Indians had withdrawn. They learned otherwise very shortly for, nearly back
to the timber, keen ears heard them and bullets came cutting
through the grass around them. There was nothing to do but
press flat, hardly breathing, until the shooting stopped, then
they tried it again and got back to the command with the
water.

The Indians lay in their own positions around the timber,
sleeping in relays for they had also undergone an agony of
strain since before daylight of the previous day. Those who

remained awake did little shooting, and they could hear sounds like crying that now and then came from the timber. Then, somewhere in the afternight, messengers slid among them with word from Ollicut that all but a few scouts left to watch the soldiers would withdraw and join the band.

Their people were safely away by then, and these particular soldiers were in no shape to pursue them. But they were leaving eighty-three of their own to remain here forever, over sixty of whom had been noncombatants.

Even though the rest of the night passed without a shot being fired, the command refused to believe that they had been given a new lease on life. This wariness remained even after daylight, although they found they could move a little without drawing a waspish bullet. Shortly after full light, a cavalryman rode unmolested down the Trail Creek Canyon, bearing a dispatch from General Howard.

After spanking off from the Lolo Trail with four troops of cavalry to overtake Gibbon, Howard had reconsidered and slowed his march to the pace of his foot troops, although remaining at some distance ahead of them. Not hearing from Gibbon, he had finally sent a courier forward to present his compliments, report on his position, and inquire as to the colonel's situation and health.

Gibbon, who at least had a capacity for pressing matters, was too exhausted from strain and drained by his thigh wound to fill the air with blue smoke as he might have done otherwise. He returned the general's compliments by the same courier and suggested tactfully that he bestir himself, getting the horse troops forward immediately and the rest up on the double.

Presently there was a stir of excitement when an Indian was seen watching from a point higher up the mountain, and the sorely punished command wheeled back into posi-

110 | Thunder on the Mountain

tion to fight again if it must. But nothing happened, and a little scouting disclosed that, except for a few lookouts, the Nez Percés had gone bag and baggage down the Ruby Creek trail toward the Big Hole River. Pursuit by Gibbon was out of the question, so he set the command to work cleaning up the field. The toll was appalling—three officers and twenty-eight enlisted men killed and thirty-eight wounded, including himself. Catlin's volunteers had been shot up badly, also, with six killed and four wounded, and the scout Bostwick was dead.

"Well, this is once it cost them something," an officer told the colonel.

John Gibbon was a rough man who was not above brutality when it seemed to be his duty, but he could think straight. Fresh Indian graves told him that the Nez Percé loss had been heavy. But in the very nature of the attack, most of their casualties had occurred in the first onslaught against the sleeping village, and that meant that many of those knocked out of the war had been noncombatants. Not only had the rest recovered from that staggering blow, they had turned the tables within the hour and inflicted a toll far heavier than the timber fight could have cost them. So he only grunted at the officer's attempt to comfort him.

The dead were gathered and buried in the timber, the surgeons did what they could for the wounded, and the supply train got in just before sundown. Howard came up with his cavalry the next morning, his four troops greatly enheartening the mauled Seventh Infantry. Gibbon was glad to return the pursuit of the hostiles to the Columbia Department, and the next day he departed with half his command to transport the wounded back to Deer Lodge. The rest of the Seventh was turned over to the plodding but persistent general.

CHAPTER ELEVEN

TOWARD THE BLOODY PLAYGROUND

Gibbon's thumping defeat in the Big Hole Valley sent out a shock wave that reverberated in the Division of the Pacific and the office of the Commanding General of the Army, where William T. Sherman was absent on an inspection tour of Northwest forts. Contrary to the rumor that spread over the scene of hostilities, however, the lanky hero of the Civil War was not coming out to take personal command of the campaign, but to combine official business with personal pleasure, arranging meanwhile to keep in contact with developments in the Indian war. Five years earlier, the northwestern corner of Wyoming had been made into Yellowstone National Park, which had become a fashionable vacation spot for the hardy and adventurous, and Sherman and his party planned an excursion into the park when they reached that vicinity. Neither Sherman nor the Nez Percés knew they were moving head on toward each other.

Momentarily the spotlight had swung back to Oliver Otis Howard and the men and officers on whom once more rested the responsibility for ending the bloody trouble. They had marched over three hundred miles since leaving the Kamiah crossing, and Howard's snailing pace had been wearing. They knew the press criticized him severely for not using his cavalry more promptly and effectively, and they shared this opinion.

Now, after the Big Hole battle, they were witnessing the same performance that had followed the fight on the Clearwater. The cavalry was again within easy striking distance of the hostiles, but the general refused to use it, insisting that he have his entire command in contact before he struck at all. It occurred to the command, if not to Howard, that, most of them being foot troops, they would have to go some to come up on the extremely mobile Indians in one body. By August the fifteenth, when the command left the Ruby Creek camp, the Nez Percés were already five days ahead.

There had been a lot of details for the general to attend to, naturally. Supplies and baggage had been transferred from wagons to pack mules again. A courier had been sent off to General Wheaton, turning back his Clark Fork column. A company of Bannocks had been recruited to act as scouts through the rough and unfamiliar country ahead. There were Sabbaths to observe, sermons to preach, and innumerable reports to write.

In various division offices, however, there was considerably more action, and orders went to Nelson A. Miles, a much more successful Indian fighter, in his cantonment at the juncture of the Tongue and Yellowstone rivers. Two days after Gibbon's defeat, Miles was in motion. A steamboat had just come up the Yellowstone with military stores, and the colonel requisitioned it and sent Samuel D. Sturgis, with six troops of his Seventh Cavalry, paddling up the river as far as the steamer could go, which was the mouth of the Big Horn. Thereafter Sturgis was to proceed overland at all speed to the northern side of Yellowstone Park, where he would intercept the Indians and give them battle when they emerged from the park into Montana again, as Miles believed they would do.

Yet another group was heading for the scenic spot on the headwaters of the Yellowstone—a party of civilians bent on escaping the Montana heat. They were George F. Cowan, an attorney in Radersburg, his wife Emma, her thirteen-year-old sister Ida, and Frank Carpenter, her brother. With them were four men friends and a cook. They had nearly reached the park when they were warned of the Indian danger, which failed to impress them, and they went on up the rugged mountain trail into a place in history.

Of all this the fleeing Nez Percés knew nothing. The thing that had happened at the Place of Ground Squirrels had left them embittered as never before, for there was no family that had not lost a loved one, and they were no longer inclined to be temperate with those who got in their way.

The wounded had to be carried on travois, which was very hard on them, and no day passed that did not see burials beside the trail. Some of the wounded, unable to endure it longer, simply fell out to accept whatever fate befell them, although none were abandoned deliberately. The march had been hard on the ponies also, the nearly three thousand head that had come out of Idaho having shrunk to a bare two thousand, and as the Indians came up the Big Hole River into ranch country they set out to acquire more.

"Let the Montana people take the blame," Joseph told his chiefs. "We asked them for peace and they gave us war, so we will go by the rules of war and take what we need."

The band had been joined by Lean Elk, an undersized man with a powerful voice who was well known to the white people as Poker Joe because of his fondness for gambling. He brought with him twenty lodges and had been in the buffalo country when he learned of the war. His booming voice made him a good commander, and he was soon in the forefront, taking his place with White Bird and Ollicut in leading the young men.

The first horse raid was made on the Montague-Winters ranch, twenty-five miles west of the mining camp of Ban-

nock, in which Montague and three others were shot and
killed. In return Indian lookouts and scouts were now fired
at on sight by white parties they drew too near. But the
Nez Percés persisted, and other and less bloody raids continued until they had added 250 ponies to their herd.

The band moved steadily southward to the headwaters of
the Big Hole River, then crossed the Beaverheads, moving
west, into the Lemhi Valley of northeastern Idaho. There,
on Birch Creek, an advance party came upon an unexpected
and tempting prize of horses, mules, and supplies.

North of them was the mountain town of Salmon, Idaho,
and toward it there moved a large jerkline outfit loaded with
general merchandise consigned to George L. Shoup & Company, coming in from the railroad in Utah. The lead wagon
and trailer were drawn by eight fine horses, and behind
came two two-wagons-and-trailer hookups, each pulled by
sixteen mules. Besides the three freighters, five passengers
were aboard, two of them Chinamen. In the brisk fight that
followed the discovery, all the white men were killed except
one passenger who escaped, and the two Chinamen were
captured.

This prize of war proved a mixed blessing. The horses and
mules were added to the pony herd, and the Indians helped
themselves to the groceries and clothing, but a third item
caught the eyes of too many, a substantial shipment of
kegged whisky. They removed a generous quantity of this
also, after which the wagons and their loads were burned,
and the two Chinamen were set free. Many of the warriors
were soon drunk and quarrelsome, and fights broke out
among them in which two of them were wounded by bullets
and another stabbed. When Joseph heard of the whisky
he ordered it dumped, after which order was restored.

The band went down the valley of the Lemhi until Heart

Mountain was reached, whereupon it swung east along the southern slope of the rising land mass that carried the Continental Divide from there to the Wyoming mountains. The band crossed the stage road connecting Utah and Montana. On the ninth morning after leaving the Big Hole battleground it crossed Camas Creek and proceeded on through the day to a good campground, now having drawn close to Targhee Pass on the western edge of Yellowstone Park, which the Indians called the geyser land.

There in early evening a scouting party rode in from the rear with electrifying news. General Howard had achieved what had seemed impossible to nearly everybody. He had almost closed the gap and was less than a sun's march behind, encamped at that moment on Camas Creek, which the Nez Percés had crossed only that morning.

The young chiefs, who had rushed up to learn the tidings, were excited and eager.

"It is now their turn!" White Bird said in a voice weighted with feeling. "While they sleep we will show them how it was with us at the Clearwater and the Place of Ground Squirrels! Make ready, my warriors!"

"Wait!" Joseph snapped out the command. White Bird whirled and stared at him in sullen disappointment. Ollicut and Poker Joe appeared let down. But Joseph paid them no heed while he pondered. He knew of the Bannock scouts Howard had employed, so the one-armed general must know where this village was located. So taking away a force large enough to give battle to the soldiers could prove disastrous for the families. On the other hand, Howard had come dangerously close to the band, which could not be tolerated. "We must deal with them," he agreed, "but not to fight them if we can help it."

Poker Joe's deep voice boomed out. "Then what?"

"We will try to steal their horses and pack mules."

Ollicut, the most reasoning of the younger chiefs, began to nod his head. "That is good," he said. "Without them the one-arm cannot march and we will get well ahead of him again."

The others soon understood, and the daring of the venture appealed to them strongly.

Joseph made a brief summary of his plan. They would go in force but would leave enough warriors behind to protect the village. They would ride slowly to the upper length of Camas Creek, then turn southwest and follow the stream toward the grassy stretch known as Camas Meadows where Howard had camped to graze his stock. The Indians would try to steal the animals in the after part of the night, when the soldiers would be sleeping the soundest and the sentries would be drowsy.

Shortly after nightfall the raiding party started out at an easy gait. No one was permitted to talk or smoke his pipe. Although it was not his practice to go along on such raids, Joseph was in command, for this one was both important and ticklish. He had divided the warriors into two parties of about fifty each, one under White Bird and Poker Joe, the other to be led by Ollicut and himself. But for the time being they rode together, their sharp eyes giving them their bearings in the faint shine of stars. Their slow, quiet pace brought them to Camas Creek in the early morning, and they turned downstream along the willows of the creek. A range of hills soon rose to the right, and out from it slid a broken flat of sagebrush and lava rock.

Joseph called a halt when they were about a mile east of the soldier camp, crossed the creek alone, and rode forward to a low butte. The country he soon saw below him was a continuation of that behind. The woodsy creek curved along the base of the line of hills to a point a little down from him where it turned sharply south across the big meadow, and this curve looped around the tents of the encampment. On the flat between him and the tents he could see the pack mules and, beyond them, the cavalry horses. Satisfied, he returned to the warriors and thereafter sat watching the heavens until the morning star emerged to show him it lacked but an hour until daylight.

At a motion of his arm the two parties separated, White Bird and Poker Joe leading their men down the left side of the creek, Joseph and Ollicut going down the opposite. When in position to start driving the animals, White Bird was to wait until the party across the creek had got in behind the camp and created a diversion. Joseph's own party rode on in stealth around the curve of the creek and across the stream from the tents. Abreast of the encampment they tied their ponies on the blind side of the trees and, carrying the rifles and carbines and revolvers they had picked up on other battlefields, they moved forward into the cover of the creek trees.

A voice cracked out in English, which they all understood. "Who goes there?"

Joseph gave a soft command, and the closer warriors shot at the point from which the sentry had called the challenge. Other sentries on this side of camp yelled back and forth, then they bolted and went racing for the camp, shouting in unmilitary alarm.

"Indians! Along the creek—Indians!"

A bugle sounded, and the warriors continued firing to add to the confusion. On the flat beyond the camp, White Bird's waiting warriors swooped in on the mule herd, firing their guns and sending the frightened animals on a pellmell rush up the creek. Warriors streaked along on the flanks to guide

the mules, while others cut in behind the cavalry horses only
to discover that they were all on picket. They managed to
cut a few ropes and send the horses scurrying after the
mules, but by then a hot fire came from the soldier camp,
to which they were too close, so they gave the horses up and
concentrated on the flying mules.

Bullets also whacked across the creek at Joseph's party in
the willows, and they returned the fire, bent on keeping the
command confused and pinned down until the stolen stock
was well away. Joseph held this dangerous position for nearly
half an hour before he ordered his braves to withdraw.
Remounted, they swung back up the creek, riding fast, and
as they did so the day's first light cracked the sky over the
Rockies.

Bugle calls came bucketing out of the camp again, and
in the strengthening light Joseph saw that he was to be
followed. He sent part of his warriors on forward to help
control the mules, which had been crossed to the other side
of the creek, and wheeled the rest of the warriors around to
turn back the soldiers. These braves he dismounted, placing
some in the rocks and brush along the base of a big hill
hugging the creek and scattering the rest on a little mound
downstream from it and beyond the trail where it came
up from the ford. Between these points a canyon ran into
the broken line of hills, and he sent the Indian ponies up
this with a small guard.

The soldiers' camp was about a mile down from this position and plainly seen in the waxing light. But it took time
for the cavalry to saddle, mount, and form into troops.
Eventually three such troops were ready and moving across
the wide flat at a gallop, the morning sun sharp in their
eyes and glinting on their equipment. The Indians watched
dust boil up and roll toward them, and they let the lead

troop hit the ford and splash over, then the warriors on the mound sent a vicious fire into their flank while the Indians on their front opened up on them.

The bugler went out of the saddle, but the rest of the troop broke apart and went crashing into a detached stand of willows on their right. The Indian fire was so hot it prevented the following troops' riding on into the ford, and these wheeled over behind the trees, halting to mill in bewilderment.

The Indians whipped a steady fire into the woods, and presently the other troops came forward on the blind side of the woods and slipped into them to join their comrades. In answer, Joseph sent forth a raven's call that brought men off the mound to slide in on the soldiers' rear. Once more they had an army command surrounded in a patch of timber.

The shooting was audible at the camp, but it took a while for the foot troops to figure out what had happened. Yet presently companies were forming up, for the shooting showed there were a lot of hostiles, and soon some infantry and foot artillery were slogging off through the sage and lava scabs to lend help. Their approach caused the Indians south of the woods to withdraw and recross the creek, taking up their previous position on the stony mound. Once the foot troops had slid into the woods, now assaulted on only two sides and affording them and the dismounted cavalry good cover, they showed no further aggressiveness themselves.

No more reinforcements could be sent out from the camp without leaving precious stores and equipment unprotected. Had they been available they would have done little good, for the position Joseph had selected was excellent for defense, although handicapped for offense, being higher than the willow woods and heavily strewn with boulders. A

combination of rocks and trees likewise protected the soldiers, and the sun climbed the sky while the two sides sent
a harrowing fire at each other, most of which was ineffectual.

But Joseph's purpose had not been to win a battle. Shortly
after noon, when he was assured that the pack mules were
safely in his own hands, he ordered a withdrawal. The Indians slipped away up the canyon to their waiting ponies
and struck out to the east, only two of them slightly wounded.

When he reached his village the mules had arrived, and
his people were in a mood of rejoicing. But he wasted no
time listening to their compliments and gave orders that the
camp be broken immediately. He had to put as much distance between himself and Howard as he could manage
while the general was immobilized.

CHAPTER TWELVE

THE GEYSER LAND

If ever the devout general felt like swearing, it must have been that afternoon of August the twentieth when he found himself set down by the Indians who had already embarrassed him before a closely watching nation and his army superiors. But there was nothing to do but file his report and try to repair the damage the loss of 150 pack mules had done to his huge command.

Yet that was scarcely half his problem. The incorrigible Nez Percés had led his foot troops on a big circle in Idaho that had worn them down, then over the Bitterroots and up the valley of the Bitterroot River, then over the high pass of the Rockies, then on another looping march into Idaho, then up here to this remote and desolate spot on the Divide, a total distance of over five hundred miles.

He had not been very foresighted in the matter of supplies, and now the foot troops were completely exhausted and on the verge of going hungry. The high country nights were cold, even in August, the water buckets freezing before morning, and they didn't have enough blankets and no overcoats. Their shoes and clothing were shot again, and the huge Indian herd had grazed off the grass until the cavalry horses, which were still in his hands, were as gaunt and tenderfooted as the soldiers.

He had already reported this fact to his superiors only to receive a stinging telegram that said, "Where the Indians can subsist the Army can live." That was less than palatable, coming from high straps who had never seen the country in which the command was operating.

One way or another Howard got the command on to Henrys Lake, almost on the Continental Divide and just short of Targhee Pass, and there he went into camp. He had barely reached that point when another dispatch arrived telling him to continue the pursuit at once or turn the expedition over to a younger, more energetic officer.

"Jehoshaphat!" Howard said finally, startling the officers who heard him.

But his built-in patience was quickly restored, and he set about remobilizing the command. He had come on to Henrys Lake for more reason than that it was a beautiful spot in which to rest. It lay immediately under the Divide, north of which were the headwaters of the Madison River. These flowed down into Montana, and the river was skirted by a rough road to Virginia City.

The general proceeded to the mining town and bought up all the groceries, clothing, and shoes the local merchants could furnish. He managed to secure a number of wagons, a few pack mules, and a considerable herd of wild Montana broncos. Meanwhile the men rested by the sylvan lake, which was covered by geese, ducks, cranes, gulls, and pelicans, and the Bannock scouts ranged forward toward the geyser land. Ostensibly they were searching for the Nez Percés, and once they returned with a few scalps that, despite their boasts, came from wounded members of the fugitive band who had been forced to fall out by the trail. On reaching camp with these trophies the Bannocks put on a big scalp dance that the troops watched with interest.

Finally, on August the twenty-ninth, the command moved forward again on the Indian trail, this time nine days in the rear.

Meanwhile Colonel Sturgis had reached a point on Clarks Fork of the Yellowstone (not to be confused with Clark Fork of the Columbia along which General Wheaton had marched) and gone into camp in order to head off the Nez Percés when they emerged from the park. He had, besides his six troops of the Seventh Cavalry from the Tongue River cantonment, a company of Crow scouts picked up at their reservation. He had also hired as guides several civilian prospectors, for he was in unmapped country with which he had had no personal experience. His and Howard's commands, each of which tripled the fighting strength of the hostiles, were about a hundred air miles apart, and somewhere between them was the quarry no one had yet cornered.

The country between was such as to give both white and red men plenty of trouble. The Nez Percés had entered it through Targhee Pass immediately after the Camas Meadows fight and moved on up the Madison headwaters. From that point the trail, with which countless trips to the buffalo country had made them familiar, curved northeast toward the Yellowstone falls. Thereafter it skirted the canyon of the Yellowstone to the mouth of an east fork that came to be called the Lamar River. This latter stream was followed by the trail to Soda Butte Creek which carried it out of the park in its northeastern corner. Once Clarks Fork was reached, there was a fairly easy descent onto the plains of eastern Montana.

Joseph had been wily enough to foresee that, if yet more soldiers had been mustered against him in Montana, they could sell be waiting for him somewhere along this well-known Indian trail. So, soon after entering the park, he turned the band south up the Firehole River, striking boldly into country with which he and his people were not familiar themselves. In this he relied heavily on Poker Joe, who assured him that once they had reached Yellowstone Lake he could lead them on to Clarks Fork over a lesser hunting trail that came out well south of the main route. This would not only evade possible soldiers ahead, those in the rear would not be able to follow through such rough, roadless country without great trouble.

Even Poker Joe was unfamiliar with the country between the Madison and Yellowstone Lake, and this caused Joseph to pull a curious switch, providing history with a rare instance of a white man's having to guide a band of Indians through a western wilderness.

The Firehole flowed north and came down from the geyser basins that already were attracting tourists. In the lower basin, when the Indians entered the park, were three such parties, camped fairly close to each other. The farthest camp north, and about three miles up the Firehole from the Madison, was that of William H. Harmon and John Shively, prospectors returning from the Black Hills who had stopped here for a few days of sightseeing. Above them was the Cowan party, which had come up from Radersburg to get out of the August heat, and uppermost was the camp of General W. T. Sherman, who had come out from Washington by way of Fort Ellis.

On the morning of August the twenty-third, the Cowans ran into members of the Sherman party who informed them of the latest military intelligence received by the general, which concerned the fight and Gibbon's thumping defeat in the Big Hole basin. Nothing was known of the Nez Percés' subsequent movements, but the civilian guide with Sherman allayed the Cowans' natural fears with assurance that as long as they remained in the geyser basin they would be safe. Even if the Indians passed through the park, they would not come that far south.

That same afternoon the prospector, Shively, who was an old man, called at the Cowan camp and he, too, was unperturbed by what they told him about the Nez Percés. Yet Mrs. Cowan remained uneasy, and when her husband rode up to the Sherman camp to seek the opinion of the general himself, it was to discover that the Washington party had, for all its reassurances, broken camp and left the basin. That was enough for the Cowans, who decided to start home themselves the next morning.

John Shively felt no such fear. He returned to his camp around five in the evening and, his partner absent on a jaunt, began to chop wood for the supper fire. The first warning he had of trouble was when two Indians, who had slipped up behind too quietly even for his keen ears, grabbed his arms and pinned him.

"What the hell is this?" Shively yelled, when they had taken his sixshooter and released him. "What're you fellers doin' here, anyhow?"

He shouldn't have been so surprised, and he got no direct answer. He was forced to mount his horse, then was whisked off down the river to the oncoming band, where Joseph assured him he would not be hurt as long as he cooperated. The Indians wanted to be shown the way to Yellowstone Lake, which Shively said he knew. He agreed to guide them, having very little choice in the matter.

Resentful as he was of the Big Hole attack on his families, Joseph had not reached the point of seeking revenge. But this was not true of many of his people, and some of them regarded the white prisoner with open hatred. This simmering rage fired the hearts of the warriors, especially. Joseph

could not curb them too tightly without risking a division in
his band that could weaken it in the imponderable struggles
to come. Yet he gave stern orders that the white man was
not to be molested. They needed his guidance to reach the
lake they must find without taking the time to scout the
strange country for themselves.

As darkness rolled in on the Cowan camp, the men of the
party sought to keep up the spirits of Mrs. Cowan and young
Ida Carpenter. They had a violin and guitar along and sat
around the campfire, singing songs, clowning, and joking.
This served its purpose, and they all went to bed enheartened
but nonetheless eager to terminate this pleasant sojourn
early the next morning.

The other men were the first up, shortly after daylight.
Cowan, his wife, and her sister were still in the tent they
occupied when into the camp rode five Indians. This was a
scouting party from the hostile encampment which, un-
known to the white people while it enjoyed its musical
evening, had been set up only a mile down the river from
them.

A. J. Arnold, who was cooking breakfast, was the coolest
of the men outside. Without turning a hair, he straightened
from his task and said, "Well, now, good morning." The
Indians had dismounted and were coming toward him,
staring with rock-hard eyes. Going to meet the one in the
lead, he offered his hand. The surprised Indian took it, and
some of the hostility left his face and those of the other
warriors.

"I've heard a little about you fellows," Arnold resumed.
"You've come a long ways and I guess you're hungry. How
about something for your breakfast?" Without waiting for a
reply, he began to hand out some of the nearby supply of
sugar, flour, and bacon.

Cowan had a different attitude, and he stepped out of his tent, angrily objecting to parceling out their limited stores, which had to last them all the way back to civilization. That turned the tide the other way, and the whole party was taken prisoner.

The vacationists were accompanied by a two-seated carriage, a baggage wagon, and four good saddle horses. They were told to break camp and pack up, which consumed quite a little time, then they were started down the river. It was the direction they had expected to travel that morning but under more reassuring circumstances.

Not knowing how close he was to capturing the Commanding General of the United States Army also, Joseph had left the Firehole and turned east up a creek that came down from Mary Mountain. The tourist party was escorted along in the rear of the Indian families for some two miles. Then, due to fallen timber on the climbing trail, the buggy and wagon had to be dropped, with their occupants transferred to the horses. The little cavalcade went on for another ten miles, coming up with the main band when it stopped for its noon camp on the slope of the mountain.

The only chief the tourists saw, even then, was Poker Joe, who spoke good English. He told them that probably, if they would give up their horses in exchange for worn-down Indian ponies, they would be released. But he warned them that some of the Indians now carried a very bad feeling toward the white people, and there would be objections to letting them go free.

Poker Joe vanished, and after a time the band moved on toward the summit of the mountain. Then the subchief reappeared to tell the Radersburg party that it was as he had hoped. If they would accept the horse trade, they would be released. The tourists were all too glad to agree, and presently, mounted on half-dead Indian horses, they started back down the mountain.

They had gone only a couple of miles when they realized that another Indian party was coming up behind them, and the manner of the oncomers betrayed at once that they were some of the ones with bad feeling. Two men of the tourist party immediately took off into the timber, and shots rang out from the Indians. Cowan slumped and fell from the saddle, and his young wife swung down beside him. The rest of the men, including Frank Carpenter, her brother, made their own dash into the timber. Only the thirteen-year-old Ida remained with her sister and the wounded man.

In a moment they were surrounded. Cowan was shot in the leg above the knee, and the wound was spurting blood. Ignoring the Indians, Emma Cowan tried to do something to stop the flow, and the young girl crouched anxiously beside her. All at once they were shoved aside by an Indian. A revolver shot rang out, and Cowan's head fell back, blood streaming from under his hat and running over his forehead. Frank Carpenter came back then to join his sisters, and once more the three of them were moving along in the rear of the hurrying band of Indians as prisoners.

The Nez Percés were having a rough time getting over the summit of Mary Mountain. Shively, the old prospector, was abiding by his agreement to guide them, but he could not take the rigors out of the trail. The herd of loose ponies crashed along ahead of the band, wearing out the old men and boys who tried to manage it. The pack animals kept wedging their packs between trees and holding up the march. But at last the summit was crossed, and beyond it the timber thinned and opened in frequent meadows. At dark the band came to an extensive valley and made camp.

There was an argument then over who was to have

custody of the white captives, which resulted in their being taken away from the warriors who had recaptured them. Afterward they found themselves being taken through the camp and, grieved as she was by her husband's fate, Emma Cowan began to fear for herself and even more for her adolescent sister. To her horror, presently, Ida was taken away by two warriors.

No great effort had been made to capture the men who had got away, which made it pretty evident who among them the warriors had wanted. To her surprise, she and Carpenter were taken to the campfire of Joseph himself. The chief did not speak to them, merely motioning to them to sit down on a blanket that had been spread on the ground. An Indian woman brought them food, and when Carpenter tried to talk to Joseph he was not answered. The cold came down, and all along the valley a hundred campfires made bright daubs in the mountain night.

The captives did not know it, but Joseph was throwing the mantle of his personal protection about them, and Ida had been taken to the camp of Poker Joe for the same purpose. That day had brought the first challenge to Joseph's authority for, although his will had prevailed when the prisoners were freed at noon, it had been defied quickly by the hot bloods who had gone after them. This was not something he could put down roughly, for unity in his people was their one hope of surviving this struggle. So now he sat with two of the captives personally through a night that presently brought rain.

Many of his people had been without teepees since the Big Hole fight, and now the deprived sat or tried to sleep under shelters of canvas or brush. Joseph had lost his own possessions, but had not used his rank to replace them from those of his people. When the rain began he had pieces of

canvas placed over the shoulders of the captives, but still
he would not talk with them.

The band moved out again in the early morning, streaming down upon the Yellowstone River. In midmorning there
was excitement, and the prisoners learned that a white
soldier had been captured and brought in. Around noon they
reached the river a little upstream from the mud geysers and
down from the source water, Yellowstone Lake. The band
forded over, finding swimming water on the far side, and
camped on the east bank to dry out and rest.

The morning's excitement had provided a new and unexpected worry for Joseph. Under questioning, the captured
soldier had disclosed that he was from a scouting detachment sent up from Fort Ellis, a military establishment near
the town of Bozeman, down in Montana. The war chief knew
that Howard was still far in the rear, but this new threat on
the left flank had to be dealt with. He thought of the hot
bloods and the desirability of getting them out of camp, and
called White Bird to him.

"You will take your best warriors," he said, "and go down
the river to the regular buffalo trail. Follow it to the east
side of the geyser land where we will join you. Look out for
soldiers, and if you see them do not attack but watch them
and send word to me. Do you understand?"

White Bird nodded eagerly. It was the kind of thing he
and his young men liked best, and it took their simmering
minds off the white prisoners. Presently he was gone with
around twenty warriors, driving north down the river. When
they were gone, Joseph ordered all the prisoners released
except for Shively, who was still needed to guide them, and
he sent Poker Joe to accompany them personally until they
were well away from the encampment.

Frank Carpenter and his sisters could scarcely believe their good fortune, and they got all possible speed out of the worn horses they were given to ride. Poker Joe advised them to leave the park by way of the Yellowstone River exit, instead of taking the longer route by which they had come up from Radersburg, making for the town of Bozeman as fast as they could travel.

So they headed northwest, aware of the danger of running into outriding parties of ill-willed Indians. In late afternoon, on coming around a timbered point, they saw in a little meadow not far beyond them a number of horses and men at what seemed to be a camp. They pulled into the timber until they could examine the scene more closely and were shortly convinced that what they saw was soldiers.

Riding on into the camp, they discovered Lieutenant Schofield and a detachment from Fort Ellis. The captured soldier had deserted them the night before, and Schofield had no idea his command was so near the Nez Percés. He was quite willing to break the camp, which had just been established, and depart with the freed captives, taking them on to Mammoth Hot Springs and safety.

Meanwhile General O. O. Howard was applying himself the best he could to close the gap between himself and the Indians. He had his Bannocks out ahead, and while they pretended otherwise they were making no effort to close with the Nez Percés, although they were a strong war party themselves. Behind them came the cavalry, jogging along and impatiently held back to the pace of the foot troops, and in the rear was the main command, uncomfortably hurried to keep up with the cavalry horses.

On the last day of August this cavalcade came dogging along the Madison headwaters toward the mouth of the Firehole. The scouts had already informed the general that the Nez Percés had turned south up the Firehole, leaving the

main and better trail. This presented a formidable prospect
for Howard and the wagons Joseph had forced him to resort
to by running off the pack mules at Camas Meadows.

It was while exploring the forecountry they might have to
pass through that the scouts came upon George Cowan,
who not only was alive but who had just completed one of
the more amazing feats of fortitude in frontier history.

Badly weakened by a leg and head wound, this thirty-five-
year-old attorney from Radersburg had recovered conscious-
ness late in the afternoon of the day he was shot by the ill-
willed Indians. His surroundings were wholly quiet, an un-
bearable thirst assailed him, and lingering ill-fortune caused
him to raise himself partly to look around just as a small party
of Indians rode by on his flank. One chanced to notice him
and drove in a bullet that gave him a third wound, this time
in his hip. He fell flat again, fully expecting them to come up
and finish him, but they were apparently in a hurry and rode
on without stopping.

He waited a long while before moving again, then managed to roll over and start crawling on his hands and knees,
since he could not stand. He wondered about his wife and
the others, but the uppermost thought in his dazed mind
was of the water his body needed so badly. He got off the
trail and into the timber where, wholly exhausted again, he
rested. Restored somewhat, eventually, he crawled on again,
and this he kept up through that afternoon and night, forcing
himself forward until spent, then crawling into the branches
of fallen trees to hide and rest.

Not until the middle of the next day did he come to a
stream that, unknowingly because of the dense brush and
timber, he had paralleled for several miles. There he threw
his fevered body into the water and finally quenched his
raking thirst. Afterward, considerably strengthened, he tore

up his underwear, made bandages, and crudely dressed his wounds. He was moving gradually downslope, and the thought came to him that if he could reach their old camp in the lower geyser basin he might find remnants of food and possibly some matches.

He managed to reach the camp, although it took three more blistering days and icy nights of crawling, and when he got there he found a few matches but no food except a handful of coffee beans. He pounded up the beans in a piece of cloth and built a fire and used an old syrup can for a pot. The can tumbled into the fire before the coffee had boiled, but he drank what was left of it.

In the afternoon of the next day, Howard's scouts found him there and, since he could not ride a horse, they left food and blankets and built a big fire for him. While he was asleep that night a high wind drove the fire into the brush, and Cowan was nearly burned alive before he awakened and managed to crawl away from it. The command arrived during the following day, and he was picked up, given the best care the surgeons could provide, and carried along in a wagon. Later that day, Arnold and Oldham, of his party, were picked up also, the latter with a slight face wound, and finally Harmon, who had been absent from camp when his partner Shively was captured.

Mary Mountain, which had given the Indians themselves considerable trouble, was enough to persuade Howard, when he reached the Yellowstone and saw that they had crossed and pressed on into even more forbidding country, that he could not keep up a direct pursuit with his wagons. The Nez Percés had made their crossing a whole week ahead of him, and the only thing he could do was turn down the Yellowstone River, along its left bank, and get back on the main and better trail.

He had been informed by then that Sturgis was on the opposite side of the park, so he sent off a courier with information as to the route taken by the Indians and his own intentions and started the big command moving down the river. This change of direction scarcely improved the going, for the wagons had to be roped down some of the hills and once the engineer officer had to build a bridge over a canyon.

Days passed while the command dogged on, and when the courier did not return Howard knew the Indians had stopped him. Another was dispatched, and he did not come back with Sturgis' reply, and the general could only hope the colonel would know where to look for what was coming toward him.

CHAPTER THIRTEEN

IT GETS A LITTLE TIRESOME

Colonel Samuel D. Sturgis needed to bow to no officer in the Army of the West when it came to an impressive record. Despite his round cheeks, curly hair, and twinkling eyes, he was a hardened campaigner who had been through the Mexican and Civil wars and gone on to win laurels in the campaigns against the Apaches, Kiowas, and Comanches. Finally he had been sent in to reorganize and take over the Seventh Cavalry that, under Custer, had been knocked to pieces in the expedition against the Sioux. But he had yet to meet the Nez Percés, whose fighting strength now numbered only a little over a hundred warriors, who were flowing through the park toward him.

As Howard suspected, none of his couriers had got through to the Seventh Cavalry's encampment on Clark Fork of the Yellowstone, having been intercepted and killed by Joseph's northern outriders. The Crow scouts, from the reservation just east of Clarks Fork, were of little more help to Sturgis than the Bannocks were to Howard, both tribes having been impressed by the strength of Joseph's medicine. Finally, the civilian scouts Sturgis had hired got into arguments with each other even, as to the nature of the country they were supposed to clarify for the colonel.

This was not surprising. The Absaroka Mountains slashed across the northeastern corner of the park region, nowhere crossed easily, and their eastern face was a dry, sterile area of broken plateaus and detached peaks and ranges. East and south lay the vast Big Horn basin, a fabulous cow country but almost entirely deserted in this section. There were only two water routes down through the breaks into Montana's Yellowstone Valley, Clarks Fork where the command was waiting and the Big Horn River farther east. One of these had to be used by Joseph in his effort to get to the buffalo grounds, where Sturgis believed him to be going, and the problem was to pick the right one.

As his second in command, Sturgis had with him Captain F. W. Benteen, veteran of the Little Big Horn disaster, a white-haired, placid, and amiable officer who had reason to respect the unlettered sagacity of the Indian. Between them, they managed to make sense of what they were told and could learn for themselves and devise a plan. A detachment under Lieutenant Scott was sent into the park and down Soda Butte Creek, along the established Indian trail. Crow scouts and a few civilian guides were fanned south, skirting the Absarokas, to probe into the passes through which the hostile Indians might come. Meanwhile Sturgis had asked the commanding officer at Fort Ellis to scout the western portion of the park in hope of discovering something more definite about the elusive hostiles.

This seemed to have paid off when word came from Fort Ellis that Lieutenant Schofield had rescued some white captives and that later Lieutenant Doan had had a skirmish with the hostiles in the vicinity of Mammoth Hot Springs. On top of that, Lieutenant Scott, of Sturgis' own command, came back up Soda Butte Creek to report another brush near the main trail farther east than Doan's encounter.

"That settles it, Captain," Sturgis told Benteen. "They stuck to the main trail, and we're set for them."

"Are we going in after them?" Benteen asked.

"No. We'll let them run into us."

This assurance lasted only a short while for, the next day, there arrived at headquarters a scout from a detachment which had been sent south. That detachment had also brushed with a party of Nez Percés, and a white scout had been killed and another wounded.

"Well, what do you make of that, Captain?" the colonel asked Benteen.

"That we know exactly as much about them," Benteen said dryly, "as we knew before we got all this intelligence."

"It appears they've split up, anyway."

"Not into equal parts, necessarily. And now they know we're waiting for them."

Sturgis nodded, considerably worried, for now there rested on his shoulders the responsibility that had weighed so unflatteringly on Howard and Gibbon, and, with the chance to surprise the Indians gone, he had to act swiftly. Two choices presented themselves. He could go in after the Indians, gambling everything on a guess, or he could build his strategy on the two routes into Montana, letting the Indians come out of the park where they chose.

The latter seemed the wiser course since he dared not split his command. So they broke camp and moved in a body to a point midway between Clarks Fork and the Stinking Water, which flowed northeast into the Big Horn River, from which he could move swiftly toward either trail into Montana. Scouts were sent out again.

At the same time a corresponding puzzle was being considered at Joseph's camp on the east slope of the Absarokas which his tired main band had reached by way of Dead Indian Pass.

White Bird and his warriors had gone ramming down the Yellowstone after leaving the main camp near the lake, considerably enlivened by being out from under Joseph's

close surveillance. Near the lower end of the canyon they
had come upon another tourist party, killing one man and
wounding another. Afterward came a slash to the northwest,
toward Mammoth Hot Springs, where a store was burned
and another white man killed.

An exchange of shots with a detachment of soldiers turned
the outriders up the east fork of the Yellowstone, where
they were supposed to go in the first place. This brought
them head on against a second group of soldiers who, apparently thinking they were risking an encounter with the
whole Nez Percé band, quickly withdrew and headed east.
Soon after leaving the park in its northeastern corner, the
outriders terrorized the mining camp of Cooke City simply
by barreling through, although the only damage they did
was to burn the stamp mill.

As instructed, White Bird had notified Joseph of the two
encounters with soldiers, and now he had a bit of luck.
Coming down Clarks Fork to the place where he was to meet
the main band, he cut the sign of a far larger military force
than he had so far encountered. The big expedition had left
the fork and headed southeast, and the outriders picked
along the trail far enough to discover, without themselves
being seen, Sturgis' new encampment. Slipping away, the
warriors had cut across the wild plateau to rejoin Joseph.

The war chief received the information that there was a
new and formidable force ahead of him with stolid resigna-
tion. The park crossing had taken much out of his punished
people, so that at times they could make only a few miles
each day. He had released John Shively at the eastern edge
of the park, giving the prospector food, blankets, and a good
horse, and he was not yet in country he knew intimately,
himself. Yet he understood the general lay of the land, and
while he smoked and pondered he began to see what the soldier chief was up to.

"They have placed themselves," he said gruffly, "where they can be ahead of us either way we might go down into Montana. That is good."

"Good?" gasped Yellow Bull. "And how is that?"

"We must make them think we are going one way while we go another."

Knowing that the new enemy would wait for him, Joseph let his people rest another day since he would have to ask much of them when they moved again. On the second morning, aware that spies would be watching, he broke camp and headed east. He continued in that direction for several hours and, when it seemed probable that the spies would have gone to inform the soldier chief that the Indians were moving toward the Stinking Water, he turned his people north toward Clarks Fork and began to hurry them.

Word reached Sturgis in midmorning that the Nez Percés were traveling leisurely toward the Stinking Water, and he moved the command into position to meet them head on when they came down upon him. But for some reason his scouts lost contact with the enemy. A wait of two days produced nothing, and it dawned on him finally that he had been gulled. He sent scouts rushing back to Clarks Fork, and when they returned to confirm his fears, for the Indian sign showed that the whole band had passed down that trail, Colonel Samuel D. Sturgis knew that he, too, had been made to look like a dunce to the ever watching public.

There was nothing to do but take off in the rear, as Howard had done so many times, and Sturgis got going. With nothing to cut communications, he was soon in contact with Howard, who was then coming up the east fork of the Yellowstone. He borrowed a troop of cavalry from the general, left behind all the impedimenta he could spare for Howard's wagons to pick up, and went pitching down Clarks Fork, some three days in the Indians' rear himself.

Yet it simply was not cavalry country. The trail was rough and winding, so that most of the time the troopers had to dismount and lead their horses, and men and beasts were soon footsore and weary. The Seventh cursed and stumbled along, harried by its red-faced officers, but none of that seemed to close the gap between them and the fleeing Indians by an inch.

The forced march was no harder on them than the forced flight was on the Indians. Day by day they staggered on, informed by their rear scouts that they were now pursued by two overwhelming nemeses. Joseph began to despair for his people. The Crow reservation was now hard on their right, but no help came from those old hunting friends and allies, some of whom were even serving as scouts for the new enemy. The ponies were giving out, but this was not all loss for his people were reduced to eating their flesh. The supply of moccasins was gone, and more and more the infirm had to be helped along by the stronger.

Night by weary night he sat by his campfire, staring into the coals and asking himself why the white man could not live in peace with the Indian. There would be no need for trouble if all men were treated alike, if they all had the same law, the same chance to live and grow. The same Great Spirit had made all people, and through him they were brothers, and since the earth was the mother of them all they should all have equal freedom upon it. The rivers could run backward as easily as a man who was born to be free could live penned up and denied the liberty to come and go where he pleased. If a man tied his pony to a stake, he did not expect it to grow fat.

He had only asked the government to be treated as all other men were treated, but he and his people were hunted like outlaws and driven from place to place and shot down like animals. If he could not take them back to their home, then let them have a home in some country where they could be free. They only asked a chance to live as other men lived, to be recognized as men. They only asked that the same law work alike on all men. If the Indian broke the law, let him be punished. If the white man broke the law, let him be punished too.

But let them be free men, free to travel, free to work, free to trade where they chose, free to choose their own teachers, free to follow the religion of their fathers, free to think and talk and act for themselves, and they would obey every law or submit to the penalty. There was only one sky above them and one country around them, and there should be one law for all. Then the Great Spirit would smile on the land and send rain to wash out the bloody spots made by brothers' hands, and no more groans of wounded men would go up to the ears of the Great Spirit.

They came down into the wide valley of the Yellowstone and reached the yellow river that flowed east and north to the Missouri, and they crossed over to the other side. They traveled east down the valley to the mouth of Cottonwood Canyon, the only break in a vertical rock wall that separated the valley from the tableland above. They stopped in the mouth of the climbing, winding canyon and made camp. When he saw the way his people moved about like the dead, Joseph wondered if he could ever take them out on the trail again.

Yet manifest destiny, in the forms of Samuel D. Sturgis and Oliver Otis Howard, had come closer than Joseph knew, for his rear scouts, too, had grown tired. The Seventh Cavalry was only a day and a half behind, with the Idaho command another twenty-five miles south of it. The men all knew they were close to the Indians again, and with a far

greater force than had ever been brought against them before. Howard's troops had learned of the steamboat waiting
at the mouth of the Big Horn to take the Seventh back to
Fort Keogh when the trouble was settled. Maybe they, or
the ones left alive of them, would go along, heading home by
way of rivers and railroads, spared the need to retrace their
tired footsteps.

For victory seemed imminent and certain. It was true that
there still was nothing ahead of the Indians, but dead horses
and stragglers along the trail showed plainly that they were
played out. Often before the Nez Percés had been able to
shoot ahead, or right or left, and get away, but there was a
limit to that imposed by human frailties. Some of the men
from the West thought of wild horses and how they could be
run down and captured by throwing in fresh relays to press
them until their strength was gone.

No one in either command was more determined than
Colonel Sturgis to close with the Indians who had slipped
through his own fingers as easily as they ever had Howard's.
His command of seven troops numbered over four hundred
men, and he had along two mountain howitzers carried by
mule pack and the usual Gatlings. When he learned in late
afternoon that the Nez Percés had gone into camp at the
mouth of Canyon Creek he ordered a forced march through
the night by men closer to the Indians' state of exhaustion
than he realized. He drove them down the fork and brought
them into the main valley the next morning. He reached the
river crossing at noon and was surprised and encouraged to
learn that the Indians had not yet broken camp. The hour
he yearned for had come.

The troopers learned that contact was just ahead, and this
released enough adrenalin to mask their fatigue. They got
over the river and re-formed and headed down the valley

beneath the bluff that shimmered in the heat and provided no way for scouts to slip up on the village by flank or rear.

Enclosed by the similar bluffs of Canyon Creek and on the edge of the Yellowstone Valley, the Nez Percés had set about breaking camp. The site was weirdly rugged, the creek lost somewhere on a wide flood plain that was empty save for dry grass and a thin stand of willows deep in the mouth, where the camp was located at a sharp bend of the canyon to the west. The shingled floor was gashed and irregular, and the heat of the Montana sun soaked into the rocks and radiated over the whole plain. The pony herd, now half the size it had been in Idaho, grazed east of the village. Tired old men, helped by boys no longer frisky, had come up to the village with pack horses. The lodges had been struck and the women were busy making packs.

This was the situation at the moment when a warrior downstream saw another waving a blanket, on down in the hazy distance, as he rode his pony in circles. It meant that soldiers had been sighted, close at hand. The message was relayed back to the chiefs just as shooting erupted outside the mouth of the canyon. The firing came from other warriors stationed down there, but soon horse soldiers swarmed into sight.

The head men's shouts cut through the popping of the guns, and a weary people reached deep in its spirit and found strength. Warriors boiled down the canyon and climbed up among the hot rocks, scarcely more than a handful, but they held the soldiers up. The rest were needed at the moment to get the village moving and to swing around the pony herd and send it driving up the canyon.

Sturgis was up front with his skirmishers, which were four of his seven troops, and Benteen was in the rear with the three other troops. One look at the situation confronting him, and the colonel had devised his attack. He hurried Benteen forward and sent him driving up the left side of the bottom to get around the village and cut off it and the horses' escape up the canyon. He dismounted his own troops and sent them running forward in a line across the wide plain. If it worked, he had the Indians bottled up.

Ignoring a peppering from the Indians in the closer rocks, he swept his binoculars over the field and saw that his luck had not been good enough. Benteen's footsore horses were making less than a spectacular charge along the western bluff, and the pony herd went thundering from sight beyond the point of rocks that marked the bend in the wide canyon.

The part of the village already packed streamed in the same direction, and other Indians were hurrying along behind on foot, abandoning what they had not had ready to take with them. Benteen nearly reached the point in time to cut some of these off, but all at once a withering, widespread fire cut into him from the point itself, where the warriors who had started the ponies had swung in to station themselves. Their assault broke Benteen's charge and sent his troops scurrying to get into better positions, and in that instant the last of the village vanished behind the point.

The closer sharpshooters disappeared simultaneously, heading for the point that protected the bend. Sturgis advanced his own men hurriedly, getting them down off the rolling ground onto the shingled bottom higher up the canyon. Yet a lesser bluff separated him from the lower plain, where Benteen was dismounting and forming his men in a line that fronted the warriors on the point. Sturgis lined his own men along this other bluff and did what shooting he could across the lower flat and over the heads of Benteen's command, but it was ineffectual.

The sun by then hung at midafternoon, and the heat had grown intense. The surge of energy in the opening phase seemed to have used up that possessed by either side. The Indians were trying to hold the point while the band made its escape up the canyon, once more slipping away from its pursuers, yet Sturgis knew that an attempt to ram past the strong rear guard on the point, in pursuit, would cost him bloodily.

The Indians might be driven off the point, and to see he detached one of his troops and sent it wheeling around to the right, past the village site and on to where it could harry the warriors on the flank and from an equal elevation. This did no good, for the Indians and rocks were one, and the sun slid down the sky with them still cemented on that obstructing point. The firing on both sides slacked off, and when night came down it stopped completely.

Sturgis brought his command back together and drew what comfort he could from the lightness of his casualties: three men killed and five wounded. He let the men eat and sleep in relays, and the slow night passed, and at daylight the rocky point was found to be deserted.

The command moved up the canyon only to discover, at a place where it narrowed, a formidable barrier of trees, rocks, and brush, completely closing the passage. Sturgis took one look at his famished, exhausted troops and footsore horses and knew that immediate pursuit was impossible. He went into camp.

General Howard caught up with him that evening and offered a rare bit of jollity.

"You know, Colonel," he said to Sturgis, "this can get a little tiresome."

CHAPTER FOURTEEN

COLLISION COURSE

The log walls of the new Fort Keogh were rising slowly, but there was little prospect of the work's being finished before a vicious Montana winter rolled in again, for mid-September had come. The busy post scarcely missed the absent troops of the Seventh Cavalry, from which nothing had been heard since they went up the river. Three more troops of the Seventh were still at the cantonment, with three others of the Second Cavalry, eight or ten companies of the Fifth Infantry, and a horde of civilian employees.

But two days after the Canyon Creek fight the building of the new post was relegated to second place, for Colonel Miles received by courier from General Howard the word that he had inherited the Nez Percé problem himself. Howard's dispatch was urgent, reporting Sturgis' failure and concluding, "The Indians are said to be going straight toward the Musselshell. I earnestly request you to make every effort in your power to prevent the escape of this hostile band, and at least hold them in check until I can overtake them."

Nelson A. Miles shifted his short-necked, sturdy body uneasily. He had counted coup on as many Indian chiefs as any other frontier commander, and he knew the country between the Yellowstone and Missouri, all of which was rolling mesa riven by deep, crooked coulees with slashing bluffs and covered by prickly pear, cactus, and sagebrush. It was treeless except for a few stringer ranges, and the cottonwood that slung itself along the banks of feeble, alkaline streams. Between the bordering rivers the Musselshell flowed east for a great distance, then abruptly curved north to the Missouri.

At that moment, Miles realized, as he tapped a brown finger on the message he had just read, the astounding Joseph would be two suns north of the Yellowstone and about 120 miles southwest of where Miles sat at his desk. The Nez Percés would follow north along an old Indian and trapper trail that ran between the Yellowstone and Missouri, with the intention of crossing into Canada for asylum with the Sioux. The Missouri badlands would compel them to cross that river at a predictable point between the mouth of the Musselshell and Cow Island Crossing, above. The colonel realized that, as of that day, he was exactly as close to these probable river crossings as was Joseph himself. Therein lay a chance to do what Howard asked.

Miles spoke curtly to the post adjutant. "Have the trumpeter sound officers' call." Then he wrote a brief summary of his intentions to send back to Howard.

The cantonment had never been as busy as it got during that and the following day. The quartermaster labored through the night loading wagons and readying horses and mules for the six troops of cavalry and four companies of infantry that were to go mounted, and in the village below the post a company of Sioux and Cheyenne scouts readied war ponies. Two more infantry companies would go along unmounted to guard the wagon train, and these footsloggers alone viewed the unexpected expedition with something short of enthusiasm.

In the following dawn, which was September the eighteenth, the command of 375 men got over the Yellowstone and up the buff sandstone cliffs on the north edge of the valley. It came out on the broken plateau and slanted its march along the general course of Sunday Creek toward the distant mouth of the Musselshell, 120 superheated miles away.

Miles rode in command, erect in the saddle, his features sharp and a little grim, his heavy hair bunching out from under his hat. He knew he was gambling on an informed guess, but this weighed on him less than something rising from the spirit of the man rather than the mind of the officer. He had been following the campaign as best he could and had conceived an outright admiration for the Nez Percé leader, whom he had never seen.

Joseph was no surly, implacable blood-letter, no roving marauder and thief, but a man of great heart and instinct. Few officers of the Army could have surpassed his generalship, and few commands could have come up with the stamina and fortitude of his people. Now it had been given Miles to destroy him, this natural prince of his people, and as an officer he had to try his best to do it.

So it was that, across the hot, bare surface of east-central Montana, an inverted V could be imagined, whose apex lay to the north at the mighty Missouri River. Each leg was over a hundred miles long, with Miles to the east and Joseph to the west, the officer knowing all too well what he had to do, the Indian in total ignorance of a powerful new force in the field against him.

The Nez Percés had emerged from the Canyon Creek fight with only three men slightly wounded, but the dragging fatigue was still on them, and they were to undergo that most enervating of experiences—the proof of falseness in old friends.

They had known of the presence of Crow scouts with Sturgis, which was not surprising since there had even been Nez Percé scouts with Howard in Idaho. But between the

Nez Percés and Crows, for ages past, there had been a close
and blood-sealed friendship. Only three years before, while
on a hunting expedition, Looking Glass and his warriors had
helped the Crows defeat the Sioux, in return for which the
Crows had paid Looking Glass great tribute and promised
him an equal service. Now Looking Glass was here, sorely
pressed, and the Crows knew it.

Since slipping out of the Canyon Creek Canyon, the
fugitive band had moved to Elk Creek and waited for the
rear guard to come in. Early on the next day's march,
Ollicut was following in the rear with a handful of warriors
when out of the haze appeared a party of strange Indians.
Realizing presently that they were Crows, he was uncertain
as to their intentions until they charged head on toward
him with blazing rifles.

The enraged warriors returned fire at once, and the wary
Crows slid off to their right. Taking a look toward the
families then, Ollicut saw a much larger party of Indians
riding to flank them. Since most of the warriors were out
on scout, there were precious few with the main band. With
a shout to his men, Ollicut went streaking forward to where
about a hundred Crows were trying to close in on the
families, riding low on the sides of their ponies and shooting
under their necks. The badly outnumbered Nez Percé warriors bored straight into them, heedless of their lives, and the
Crows broke and scattered.

Recovered from the shock of this treachery, the Nez Percés
realized that the Crows were after loot, principally horses,
and the effort was kept up through the next several suns
until the fugitives came to the valley of the Musselshell.
Joseph had learned by then that Howard and Sturgis were
both on his rear again, not pressing, with Howard over east
of their backtrail and Sturgis coming directly behind the

band. He knew the worn-down condition of both commands and did not suspect that there might be another reason for their present lack of aggressiveness.

He had reached the Musselshell at a point only thirty miles west of its sharp turn to the north. After a talk with his chiefs, he decided that it would be easier to turn up the river until they came into alignment with the gap into the Judith basin. One chief or another had been through that region on buffalo hunts, and they knew this would put them on a direct march to either of two good river crossings. One was at Cow Island, the only shallow ford in a reach of many miles. The other was a fairly easy bull boat crossing at the little town of Carroll, a receiving depot for freight brought by steamboat from the railhead at Bismarck, Dakota Territory. Once they reached the Judith gap they would have the freight road, with its waterings and bridges, to lead and speed them.

The change was made, and the band moved up the south bank of the Musselshell and onto the freight road. This brought them into a thin civilization, but none of the white people they saw were a serious threat to them. Joseph knew that Forts Benton and Shaw were not far to the west, and there could be outposts he did not know about, but the only soldiers his scouts reported were those who long had been behind him. He pressed on, and on the fifth sun after the last trouble with the Crows the band drew near Carroll.

In camp that night Joseph saw something in the faces of the young men that made him hesitate about crossing the river anywhere near Carroll, which boasted a population of seventy-five white people and usually had on hand twice that many floaters. Realizing his young warriors still yearned to avenge the Big Hole attack, he ordered the march swung west to Cow Island, fifteen miles up the river.

There had been recent developments at Cow Island of which he was unaware. This natural ford on an otherwise formidable river had for years been the head of navigation, during the fall, for steamboat freight consigned to Fort Benton and the settlements south of the fort. Recently it had also served the new outpost of the Royal Northwest Mounted Police at Fort McLeod. The day the Nez Percés turned upstream and away from Carroll, the steamboat *Benton* had unloaded at Cow Island fifty-odd tons of freight and gone back down the river. The goods were being guarded by a detachment of the Seventh Infantry from Fort Benton, twelve men under Sergeant William Moelchert. There were also four civilians present.

Fort Benton was mainly a trading post and, militarily, was only an outpost of Fort Shaw whose commanding officer, Colonel John Gibbon, had already received a threshing and thigh wound from the Nez Percés. Major Guido Ilges was at Fort Benton with seventy-five men, and he had been informed that the hostiles might soon appear on that reach of the river. But he was seventy miles west of Sergeant Moelchert. The latter, hearing of the approaching Indians, hastily dug rifle pits at some distance from the huge pile of stores stacked on the north bank of the river, so as to have a clear field of fire if he and his handful of men had to take on the hostiles.

The Indians came down to the crossing in late afternoon of September the twenty-third, the advance guard appearing first and waiting until the main band had caught up. Then about twenty warriors rode across the river, aware of the soldiers on the far bank but ignoring them. The soldiers gladly held fire, and the pack train came over. Then came the main band and pony herd, the warriors standing between them and the little tag of soldiers. The band then went on for two miles and made camp, and Sergeant Moelchert heaved a sigh that nearly carried to them. But the sergeant's relief was premature.

The people safely out of the way, the warriors wheeled back to the crossing. Some of them tied up the guard with enough rifle fire to keep them flat behind their breastworks, and the rest pitched into the stores that were needed desperately. Pack ponies were brought in and loaded with all the sacked flour, rice, beans, sugar, and coffee they could carry. There was also plenty of soldier food, hardtack and bacon, and to replace the utensils lost in the camps from which they had been driven there were pots, pans, buckets, and tin cups in abundance. Then night came down, and the Indians set fire to what stores were left and, after sending a few parting shots at the soldiers, they pulled out for camp.

That night there was much feasting and the people felt happy. Joseph shared the mood. He was across the Missouri, at least two suns' march ahead of Howard and Sturgis. So he sent runners off to Sitting Bull, just across the border on the sweetgrass prairies, to tell him that another band of red men had been forced to run from the soldiers of the Great White Father and to propose that they join forces if they were attacked.

On this same twenty-third of September, Colonel Miles reached the mouth of the Musselshell, fifty miles down the river, with his scouts, troops, and wagon train. He had tied Joseph in the race to the Missouri, although the Indian chief had widened the apex of the inverted V by choosing a crossing as far west of the Musselshell as he could get.

Miles' principal officers were all captains, Tyler who was in charge of the Second Cavalry, Hale with the Seventh, Snyder who commanded the mounted infantry, and Brotherton with the foot companies and wagon train. These five had been thrown into the struggle unexpectedly at its climax, and on them depended the outcome of three intense and bloody months of Indian chasing and fighting.

"Well, there's a good chance Joseph doesn't know we exist," Miles told his officers, "but right now we have only a vague idea of where he is. If he's coming down the Mussel-shell, we're ahead and set for him. But if he's turned toward an upper crossing he can give us the slip as handily as he did Sturgis and be over the border before we can get cracking."

They were all seasoned field officers and understood the colonel's quandary. The command could be split, and the other crossings covered, but that would weaken it danger-ously. Miles could guess again and move upstream in force, perhaps to let Joseph slip down the Musselshell behind him and get away. Like the other officers who had tried it, they were learning firsthand that outmaneuvering the Nez Percés was more a matter of intuition than of logic.

Hale was robust and venturesome, with a taste for fine horses, and he took a keen look up the shimmering river valley to the south. "Well, Colonel, the wily devils have shown a fancy for tough country so far. If they run true to form they'll come down through the Musselshell breaks. They can hardly know we're here, and that would play hob with the commands they do know about behind them."

"That's my thought," Miles agreed. "We'll wait here."

The next day the *Benton* paddled down the Missouri, putting in when the big military force was observed on the bank. The captain reported all quiet at the Cow Island crossing, as it had been when he left, and the same thing at Carroll. Reassured, Miles quit worrying, and the *Benton* slid on down to a wood landing some distance below and tied up to take on fuel. Nothing showed up by way of the Musselshell, along which Miles now had his scouts, and another day dawned serenely, a condition that was shortly shattered.

In midmorning a mackinaw boat came dipping down the river from Cow Island with word that the Nez Percés had crossed there two days before.

Miles was stunned. Cow Island was fifty miles west of him, and the Indians would now be two days north of the Missouri. He knew the river could not be crossed at this point, for one of the scouts had tried it the day before and drowned. It would take a week for the command to ferry over in the mackinaw, and the long, rough march to Cow Island would set him back at least two or three days more. That meant that Joseph would be over the border before the pursuit could even get over the river.

It had happened again.

If only he had held onto the *Benton!* Miles lifted his binoculars and turned them east and saw, off across the tawny wastes, a faint smudge of smoke rising against the sky. The steamboat was still at the wood landing, but apparently with steam up and ready to slip on downstream. A courier couldn't get there in time to stop and turn it back.

"The cannon!" he shouted. "Snyder, throw a shell or so ahead of that steamer! Quick about it!"

Officers and watching enlisted men got the idea. They had along a twelve-pound Napolean cannon and a breech-loading Hotchkiss gun. The twelve-pounder was swung into position, and in a moment the gunner sent a shell whacking into the hills beyond the wood landing. It brought no response, and they sent a second shot lobbing through the hot morning, then keen ears heard the low, carrying tones of a steam whistle.

"They got the idea!" Hale yelled. "They'll be back to see what we want!"

Miles pulled out a handkerchief and mopped his forehead, but his suspense did not subside. He not only had to get over the river. He had to intercept Joseph within the short eighty miles between the Indians and the border that meant their full and final escape into country where they could not be touched. Western Canada had not yet resorted to reservations for its aborigines and was tolerant toward refugees from across the line.

The *Benton*'s skipper had got the message and by noon had swung to and come back up to the Musselshell. The passengers were put ashore, and through the rest of the day the packet plied back and forth, setting the command on the north side. It took a lot of wearing time, and night had socked in again when it was accomplished.

In the next early dawn the column hit the trail, moving away from the river and onto the high, rolling prairies. The Sioux and Cheyenne were still riding their scrawny utility horses, their carefully groomed war ponies being driven along riderless, and they were excited by the prospect of a fight. The officers harried the command onward, and Miles dredged up all he knew about the country ahead of them.

From Cow Island Joseph would have to cross the western end of the Little Rockies, which he would do by way of Cow Creek, then he would have to bend north to come around the Bearpaws on their eastern slope. If, Miles reasoned, he could keep himself hidden by moving east and north of the Little Rockies, and if he slanted his march just right, and if he could make good enough time and the Indians did not hurry, he ought to intercept them sometime before they reached Milk River, the last stream between them and the border.

CHAPTER FIFTEEN

ONE LAND AROUND THEM

Overnight the weather turned cold, which drained off the strength that came to the Nez Percés from the stores seized at the river. The old and infirm, the women and children again found it almost more than they could manage to break camp and resume the long journey north. Freedom was so near when measured by miles, yet so far in terms of endurance. But the band got away from the river the morning after the crossing, striking toward the pass in the Little Rockies.

In midafternoon the advance scouts came upon a bull train bound north to Fort McLeod with provisions loaded two days before at Cow Island. They counted nine white men with the wagons and dismissed them as a danger to the band and, after sending back a warning, they passed off to the flank. The main band likewise skirted the freighters, wary but not wanting more trouble, yet when the warriors in the rear guard came up they saw the matter differently. They no longer needed supplies, but these were white men, and the band was safely past. They charged the wagon train.

The bull whackers had had Indians on their minds ever since they saw the first dust, then discerned the slowly marching figures in the distance. When this had passed on peacefully they had eased up and so were caught by surprise when they saw the war party whip down upon them, quartering in from the rear. It was too late to circle and prepare for a fight, and all they could do was blaze away.

The Indians lashed in from the flank to within range, shot and curled back, then circled to swoop in again. Their dust all but hid them, while the wagons were a clearly visible target. A teamster let out a yell and fell dead. When a second man dropped lifeless the remaining seven broke and ran for the nearby hills on the other side, the wagons hiding them until they were safely away.

When they realized resistance had ended, the warriors went for the wagons. The freight proved to be the type of supplies they had already obtained at the crossing, but there was whisky and the stern war chief was now well away to the north. Just as the braves prepared to help themselves to this treat, an Indian on top of the wagons took a sudden look to the southeast.

"Dust!" he shouted. "Soldiers—coming here!"

That left them no time to break into the whisky, but they managed to set fire to the wagons. Realizing presently that the soldiers outnumbered them, they raced to their ponies, sprang astride and went racing away.

The command streaming toward them was that of Major Guido Ilges. He had left Fort Benton with thirty-six mounted men the day before to protect the stores at Cow Island. He had arrived there too late but, learning of the northbound wagon train, he had put his tired command on the trail into the hills of the Little Rockies. Ilges saw the Indians break away from the burning wagons and rapped an order and took his men after them, scarcely within rifle range but exchanging furious shots.

He managed to close the gap enough that a trooper was shot dead from the saddle, and when the horse of another went down Ilges called it off. The Indians hauled around, as if about to reverse the pursuit, then themselves took second thought and disappeared into the hills. Yet they

curved back under cover of the high ground to see if these
soldiers came from the command of the one-armed general
who so long had nipped at their heels.

Joseph knew all too well that if the trail had been a hundred miles longer many of his people could never have
made it. The distance remaining was so short that he conserved them to his utmost, breaking camp later each morning, placing the day's objective less far ahead. He learned
that the soldiers who drove his warriors away from the
burned wagons were from the west and not the south, where
two large armies were doggedly following him. These were
drawing no closer to him, and he thought that by using his
people sparingly they could find the strength for a last dash
to the border if one became necessary.

Yet there was very hard going ahead, as each new day
proved. The country fell down into the Cow Creek trough,
between the Little Rockies and the Bearpaws, and the sky
stayed gloomy, and the nights grew colder still. September
was nearly over, and they moved steadily northward where
fall came earlier, slanting a little to the east to get around
the Bearpaws.

They crossed the water divide and on the afternoon of
September the twenty-ninth came to Snake Creek which
flowed north to the Milk, and all through that day the look
of the sky warned that a storm was gathering. Yet the clouds
were forgotten when it was learned that the advance scouts
had found and killed a number of buffalo, with which this
region abounded.

The only wood was brush, and it was scarce, but buffalo
chips were plentiful and the familiar smell of their burning
soon covered the campground. Joseph sat by his fire, where
his wife was cooking fresh meat, and found another of those
rare moments when life was good even though it was never

kind or certain. Here was buffalo, and to his unspoiled eyes the country was beautiful, and he had almost won his freedom and that of his people.

Many of the lodges and campfires had empty places, but they were almost in a land where they would not have to live where they did not choose. He had shown the Great Father that the Nez Percés were men. He would remain at a safe distance, and perhaps the Great Father would send some head men to him who would agree to let them come back to live in peace here in this spot where nobody else wanted to live.

It was not often that he dared to dream, and he came back to reality when Spring of the Year came up to him. He saw on her mouth the first smile that had graced it in many moons, and her breast lifted. "It is so good here," she said. "Can we not rest and make meat? The people are tired and the hoofs of the ponies are tender."

He shared her yearning but shook his head. "The runners have not come back from Sitting Bull. It must have been hard to find him. So there would be no help if we were attacked before we get to his country."

"You have fought well without him."

He let out a gusty sigh. "But we are tired, and our warriors are little more than a hundred, and there are many hundreds of soldiers behind us."

The face of his wife grew somber again but she nodded her head. "It is better to be sure," she agreed. "But it is so hard, so endless."

Evening appeared and there was feasting and rejoicing and the recounting of many an adventure along the trail almost behind. Night came with the moon lost somewhere in the sable sky.

Under that same brooding mantle, eight miles to the east

and as unaware of the proximity of the quarry as the Nez
Percés were of him, Colonel Miles bivouacked his tired
command after a forced march of sixty miles from the
Missouri River. Coyote cries ran before the wind, and in
both camps chip fires glowed and died, and dreams slid
through many minds, bringing to reposed faces quiet smiles
in the darkness.

One land now surely united them, a broken plateau of
naked hills and desert valleys that tipped gradually toward
the Milk and over which flowed the deepening cold of
autumn. The undersized willows along the feeble streams
shared the great emptiness with sage and dried grass. There
were only a few scattered ridges to break the wind and the
cutbanks of the gashed coulees.

Out of this in the late afternight came Milan Tripp,
civilian scout, who had been off with a handful of Sioux,
to awaken the commanding officer.

"Located 'em, Colonel," Tripp said quietly. "They're on
Snake Creek in a kind of hill-locked little valley and keepin'
no big lookout our way. It don't look to me like they're onto
us."

The last drowsiness was knocked from Miles' head as he
sat up in his blankets.

"Good. How far off are they?"

"Eight or ten miles. The valley's open west of their village,
and they got their hoss herd on down. Looks like a good
setup for us."

"Glad to hear that."

"We movin' out?"

"As soon as we can."

Miles rose to a stand, stretching to take a sudden tension
out of his shoulders. He walked over to arouse his adjutant
who, after a few words, moved on to interrupt the sleep

of the various subordinate commanders. There was no com-
motion, no summary bugling, but the big command was soon
up and making speedy preparations for a march that was
bound to end in the fight of their lives.

Brotherton was ordered to wait where he was with his
foot companies and the wagon train, then come up when
summoned. At four o'clock the ten companies of horse moved
out behind the Sioux and Cheyenne scouts. They went at a
rapid walk, the distance ahead of them greater than a bee-
line, for Miles wanted to circle west and come in on the
open end of the little Snake Creek valley.

The excitement was great yet controlled and quiet. Orders
were passed by word of mouth or, when a low voice would
not carry, by a motion of hand or sword, and the only sound
was the jingling of equipment and the soft hoof-falls of over
six hundred horses. The light strengthened, and the sky was
clear, and the undulating prairie offered no hindrance to a
swift and steady progress.

The Indian trail was cut at some distance south of Snake
Creek, and it threaded up and through a gap between the
low ranges of the sterile Bearpaws and a detached mountain.
The Sioux and Cheyenne, who had been driving their war
horses, halted to quit their flea-bitten ponies and mules and
strip for action and mount their best steeds. Miles rested the
remaining command while he rode forward with the civilian
scout and Lieutenant Oscar Long, his adjutant.

They went through the gap and came presently to a low
ridge where the scout motioned for the officers to dismount.
Slipping on to the top-of-land, Miles put his binoculars on
what was to be the battleground about a mile below him.

Immediately before him the falling plateau ran widely on
either hand, and beyond that an accented line marked the
imbedded course of Snake Creek. Directly forward a string

of three buttes interrupted this line, and smoke stain beyond showed that they concealed the village. The buttes
were low, separated by gaps, the central one a flattop and
the others mounds. At a distance on north ran a higher,
continuous ridge that pinched in on the creek in the east
to form a water gap. The west end was open, as the scout
had reported, and on down the valley grazed the big herd
of ponies.

A strange emotion rose in Miles and tinged his thoughts
with regret. A forced march of twelve days had brought
him to this exact point of interception against great odds and
against a mind as keen as he had ever encountered. That
gave him no satisfaction. Joseph had no telegraph to keep
him informed, no great nation behind him to supply un-
limited resources. All that he had and was lay there in that
quiet village, and it seemed unfair, even cruel, that a
nation founded on the principles he fought for should have
used so great an advantage to crush him. Something fine and
gallant had flashed across the West because of these people,
something that was dying and might one day be missed.

But Miles the officer returned to his command and at eight
o'clock, four hours after locating the fugitives, threw his
powerful force against them with all the skill and determina-
tion he could manage.

The Sioux and Cheyenne and three mounted battalions
came over the last low ridge at a trot that quickly became a
gallop. On the last descent they split, the Seventh and Fifth
striking for the open end of the village, the Second slashing
off toward the herd of horses without which the fugitives
would have to stand and fight. Still going at this pounding
pace, the Fifth and Seventh fanned out on a skirmish line,
wheeled east around the row of buttes, and came in upon
the village.

Captain Owen Hale, leading the Seventh, saw that his

cavalry handled itself better ahorse than Snyder's mounted infantry. As he came in flush with the camp, which could then be seen openly for the first time, he realized that the Indians had been partly packed up to move. Mounted hostiles could be seen hurrying off toward the horses, and a dark line drawn across the sage, between the north ridge and south buttes, indicated that a coulee had to be crossed for the command to get in on the encampment.

He was within a hundred yards of the coulee when from all along its length came a storm of bullets. He took this in while the sound crashed against him, then something more tangible hit him and he died. His horse fell immediately afterward and, on down the line, Lieutenant Biddle died in the saddle. Other riderless mounts wheeled away terrified, and this turned the whole charge into wild confusion. Hostile shooting now came from other points, and within five minutes the attack had been blunted, broken, and the two battalions driven back.

There had been a hair's width of warning for this bedeviled little band, which again had reached into the depths of an undying spirit and found strength.

Expecting to rest until midday, the camp had been serene and confident until, shortly after daylight, two scouts came galloping in from the south. They had seen a big dust, off to the east, that in view of its direction was more apt to be moving buffalo than soldiers, since none of the latter were known to be off that way. But they had deemed it well to report it, and Joseph and his chiefs decided at once that it would be wise to break camp and move on. There seemed to be no immediate danger, so Looking Glass, in charge of the marches, advised the people to take time to eat a good breakfast.

Then, about an hour later, another scout appeared on the flat-topped butte to the south, riding his pony in short

circles and waving a blanket over his head. It was the old
dreaded signal that meant the enemy was upon them, that
yet another attack impended.

A wild stirring disorganized the camp, but Joseph's deep
voice rang above the shouting of the men and the wailing
of the women.

"Enough of that! We must make ready!"

Never since the Big Hole massacre had he camped his
people without planning a defense, digging rifle pits where
natural formations did not serve the same purpose. This site
was admirably suited the way it lay. The eastern gap was
narrow, hugged by rises, while a coulee ran across the open
end. Another coulee cut along the foot of the north ridge,
while the creek's sharply carved bed hugged the base of the
south buttes. All these depressions were interconnected, two
to six feet deep and fringed with sagebrush to hide the
heads of the occupants.

When the people quieted and he heard a rumble like that
of running buffalo, he knew that the soldiers coming against
him were mounted, so their attack would come against the
open end of the village, on the west. He snapped out orders
to his chiefs, who had raced up to him.

"White Bird—Ollicut—take plenty of warriors to the
coulee west of the camp. You must stop and hold the yellow
legs. Lean Elk, take your men to the top of the north ridge
and do your fighting from there. Looking Glass, pack the rest
of the village, and move out those that are packed already,
and send a guard with them. Get the others away while we
hold back the soldiers if you can. I will take the old men
and boys to bring in more pack horses."

He watched them hurry away to obey him.

Going to his own camp, Joseph admonished his wife to
make ready with all haste, saying he would send in the

ponies she needed, and he took the twelve-year-old daughter with him to bring them in to her. Carrying rope, he went across the creek with the girl, a number of other men and boys already streaming toward the pony herd ahead of him. Would there be time? It did not seem possible.

And so it was when more mounted soldiers than he had ever seen broke over the rise to the south. They came at a gallop and split, the main part heading west to attack the way he expected. But he saw in dismay that the rest were driving toward the horse herd and the packed part of the camp, which had now moved out through the gap. A moment later this oncoming column divided again, part of it continuing toward the loose horses, the rest turning in to cut his people in two parts. Simultaneously the roar of rifle fire swept to him from the west side of the camp.

Those caught in the camp were bottled up, with him outside. Handing the rope to his daughter he said, "Catch a horse and join the others who are outside. Go with them, if they can get away, and stay with them."

She looked at him, reluctant and pleading, but he waved her on.

Intercepting a riding warrior, he took the pony and charged directly through the nearby skirmish line of the soldiers to get back to the trapped Indians. Bullets cut his clothes and his horse was wounded, but he got through unhurt.

Yellow Bull had already discovered the new attack from the east and slid warriors onto the framing slopes to stop it. Assured of that, Joseph rode on into the camp, which was now crisscrossed by bullets from the two enemy lines. His task of getting the rest of the families away rendered hopeless, Looking Glass had ordered them into the coulee behind the camp for protection.

CHAPTER SIXTEEN

ONE SKY ABOVE

Captain George Tyler, commanding the Second, had swung his battalion in on the east side of the camp with orders to run off the Indian herd and also to seal that end of the village. He wheeled in on his objective to see, out on the right, part of the band hurrying off to the east and north. There were around a hundred pack ponies with them, some fifty or sixty women, old men, and children, and he saw from the rifles and crisscrossing cartridge belts that a number of warriors were there to defend them. The escapees would be a small part of the band, Tyler knew, and he ignored them momentarily and concentrated on the loose horses.

Most of these were down the valley, but there were a few grazing on the higher ground to the north, with Indians hurriedly roping as many as they could catch. The main loose herd was the important consideration, and he sent Lieutenants McLernand and Jerome pelting down the valley to take care of them, although there were Indians in evidence there also. Then he swung the rest of the Second in toward the bluffs on the east side of the camp, only to receive as withering a reception as Hale and Snyder had got on the west side. Pulling back hastily, Tyler dismounted his men, who held onto their mounts by means of lariats, and ordered them to dig in and fight.

Meanwhile McLernand succeeded in driving the few Indians away and starting some eight hundred loose ponies careening down the valley. The troop rode in pursuit to make sure they did not fall back into hostile hands, and finally headed and swung them south into a little valley. That guaranteed that the remaining Indians could not escape, even if they fought their way out of the trap.

"Well, they're afoot," Jerome congratulated the senior lieutenant. "And it shouldn't take long to roll up the rest."

They had not had a good look at the field, which Miles had, and the colonel was not so optimistic. Coming in on the south, he and his staff had set up a command post in a seepy draw between the flattop and the mound to the west. Although dust still covered the foreground, Miles knew that his main punch had been stopped cold. Even so, he was staggered by the first report from the field, which came when Lieutenant Erickson, wounded and bloody, whirled out of the gritty mantle.

"Good God, Colonel!" Erickson gasped as he swayed in the saddle. "They're concentrating on the shoulder straps! I'm the only damned officer of the Seventh left alive!"

That was only a slight magnification, Miles soon realized. Including Erickson, every officer in that battalion had either been wounded or killed by sharpshooters who had learned to recognize and pick off the enemy leaders first.

The Seventh, now dismounted and dug in behind dead horses or hasty breastworks made of anything available, had born the brunt of the attack. Hale's K Troop, which had been the first to engage the Indians, had suffered a loss of over sixty per cent. Of the 115 men in the battalion, fifty-three were dead already. The Fifth Infantry had been badly but less severely battered, and to ease the pressure on the Seventh, Miles sent orders to the Fifth to attack at once.

Out in the blinding dust, Captain Snyder was pinned flat with this command, out of touch with most of it and aware mainly of the galling fire pouring into his position from magazine rifles in the hands of deadly marksmen in the brush-screened coulee ahead. Receiving Miles' order to attack, he called to his bugler.

"Trumpeter, sound deploy by the right flank!"

"I can't, sir," a voice responded. "I'm shot!" The bugler lay with a bullet against his spine, and when Snyder yelled to a sergeant near the wounded man to take him to the rear, the bugler answered again. "He can't, sir! He's dead!"

The battalion adjutant crawled up to Snyder, and he had a shattered left arm and one ear had been shot off. Between them they got the Fifth moving, and it went forward into a stepped-up fire that quickly drove it back.

The wounded were coming into the command post, and the surgeons found themselves with a rapidly growing hospital. One of the wounded was Captain Myles Moylan, of the Seventh, hit in the thigh. His A Troop had been in Reno's battalion on the Custer expedition and gone through the rout on the flat and the fight on the hill, and he was quick to inform Miles that he had never seen anything like this.

"And don't forget," he reminded the colonel, "that the Sioux had thousands and there's only a handful of these fellows. I wonder how it would have turned out if this Joseph had commanded the Sioux."

Presently Lieutenant McLernand rode in to report that the pony herd had been captured and was safely out of the hostiles' reach, and he remembered that there had been more horses on the north side of the field that were now gone. Obviously they had been taken by the Indians who had escaped with a pack string, and he asked and received Miles' permission to overtake the fugitives and return both them and the horses.

Things had gone pretty well for McLernand so far, and

he led his troop out in confidence, running freely down the valley. He had gone some five miles before he overtook the fleeing little band of Indians, with about a hundred loose ponies being moved along on their flank. The warriors with the people saw the troop at the same time and wheeled about, ready to fight.

It looked obvious that the Indians could not be captured without a bloody brawl with the noncombatants in the thick of it. McLernand also remembered the wounded back at the command post and the reports coming in from the field. The idea of attacking looked wholly unattractive, but there was a chance to get at the loose horses, which were off to the right.

So G Troop slanted off and hooked around the ponies and headed them back up the valley. This was barely accomplished when the warriors came boiling after them, shooting as they rode. McLernand had all he could do to fight them off and hold onto the horses and get back to the main body intact.

By midmorning, with casualties still piling up, Miles knew he had to find another way to handle this. He was not only nailed down completely by the Indians in the coulees and making no progress. The Indians on the east bluff were pretty well occupied by the Second, but a contingent on the north ridge was free to sharpshoot at will. Yet others lurked outside the lines, which he realized when he tried to get water for the wounded and the detail sent down the creek with canteens was driven back. He had to get possession of the high points himself, which would let him fire more effectively into the coulees and cover the upper part of the creek so there would be access to water.

The probable cost was sobering but it had to be attempted, and he pulled out part of the Fifth and moved it around the field to support the Second, which the Indians on that side still kept nailed down. The men rose to the occasion and stormed the stronghold ahead and above them and bought with blood every foot they gained. It slowly grew clear that there were only about thirty Indians up there, widely spaced, yet every time the troops tried to advance these few soon stopped them.

The weight of numbers had to tell and little by little the Indians withdrew, going north along the ridge where the sharpshooters were located, and at last the troops were in possession of their objective, the east bluff above the creek. This brought the dividend Miles had expected, for from the new position the Second and Fifth could enfilade the Nez Percé line, now strengthened, along the whole north ridge.

Tyler and Snyder fell to with vengeance and gruelingly occupied that position too, sending the Indians squirming down through the desert brush and grass to the coulee behind the village. Although soon secure, the new position was not to be comfortable for the troops, for the fire that now swept up from below was as seering as it had been before when it swept down. A sergeant discovered that when, peering over the rim for a look, he had his hat and a lock of hair shot from his head.

Yet the maneuver had eased the pressure on the weakened west flank and distributed it evenly around the field. It also let the command get to water, and Miles gave James Snell, a civilian scout, a string of horses to carry it to the wounded and the men in the lines. Snell made his rounds, exchanging full for empty canteens, and ironically the sky darkened and threatened a rainstorm that would supply water in wholly unwelcome quantities.

When the lines had been thinned enough to cover the south buttes also, Miles knew he had the Nez Percés bottled completely for the first time in the campaign, but he was far from easy about the outcome. It was ten to one Joseph had sent runners to Sitting Bull, who could be here anytime if he chose to take up arms again against his old enemy. If that developed, nothing could keep the Custer massacre from happening all over again, but it was a danger he had to ignore.

Noon came and the troops, sprung from a punctual people, munched hardtack and the lean strips in their raw bacon and began to notice an increasing chill in the air. With the Indians centralized and submerged in the coulees, it was possible to bring in the men too gravely wounded to walk and make some effort to collect the dead. The fight for the high ground had added greatly to the cost of the day's inconclusive gain. That persuaded Miles to resort to a siege until Howard and Sturgis could arrive. Each had a command equal to or larger than his own, although God knew how many miles away they were.

But there was one more thing Miles wanted to accomplish badly enough to pay the price. The Indians had access to the length of creek running past their camp, and it would speed things up if he could cut them off from that. At present the village itself was deserted, the noncombatants hiding in the coulees, but once night fell they could slip back in for food and blankets. If he could prevent that by burning the village and could seize and hold that length of the creek, cold, thirst, and hunger would become his allies.

The Seventh still held the open west end of the field, confronted by a screened coulee that all day had poured forth death. But warriors must have been withdrawn from there and sent to the north and east sides after the heights were lost to them, and on this probability Miles built his tactics. At one o'clock three companies of the Fifth Infantry

were withdrawn from the north and east. Under Romeyn
and Carter they were remounted and sent on a feint down
the valley. It would appear to any watching Indians, Miles
hoped, that they had gone in pursuit of the escaped pack
train.

When this had been done, the rest of the Fifth and the
Second Cavalry opened an enormous fire on the coulee and
broken ground below them, indicating an intention to charge.
Under cover of this, the departed troops wheeled and came
streaking back up the valley. The west coulee would
probably have been thinned further yet to meet the expected attack from the bluffs. This would let the arm sweeping up the valley drive across to the village and destroy
it, then swing over to the cutbanks of the creek. These, in
turn, would provide a natural fortification that would hold
the water the Indians could not long go without.

The Seventh parted to let the mounted charge go through,
and the three companies of the Fifth swept by them and
almost to the west coulee before they realized that it had not
worked as planned. A fire nearly as deadly as that which
decimated Hale's battalion there cut this one to pieces also,
and Romeyn, shot through the lungs, was one of the first
to go out of the saddle.

Only Carter and fourteen men of his Company I got
through to the edge of the village, but before they could do
any burning they were themselves scorched by rifle fire.
Five of them fell, while the rest bolted to get into any cover
they could find. The village remained intact, and nobody
had come even close to the desired reach of the creek, and
when Miles heard the casualties had been thirty-five per
cent he called off the whole sally.

It was then three o'clock and all at once things grew quiet
enough for the men to notice that it had begun to rain. A

gray mantle over the distant mountains indicated that, up
there, the moisture fell as snow. Teeth already chattered, and
over at the hospital the wounded had neither shelter nor
blankets.

Through with assaulting what appeared a perfect trench-
works, Miles moved his artillery to the northeast buttes.
A rider and two mules were killed in getting it there, but
it soon began to lob shells into the coulees. Worried by the
rain and threatened snow, which soon could make the
country impassable, he got off a dispatch to Howard urging
him and Sturgis to hurry, and another to Brotherton, back at
their camp of the night before, ordering him up with the
wagon train.

Dusk arrived prematurely and came as raven clouds bearing snow. This soon fell on the bluffs where troopers lay
in thin battle jackets, on the unsheltered wounded, and on
the kidney-shaped depression of some six acres where 450
Nez Percés lay hidden. Nearly three-fourths of these were
women and children, for many of the older men and boys
had been out after horses when the fighting started and had
got away with the escapees.

Those remaining were without food or blankets to protect
them from the cold. Contrary to Colonel Miles' assumption,
these items had mostly gone off in the pony packs, so it
would have done him little good had he succeeded in burning the village. In that last bloody fight, the warriors had
sought only to retain their water, which they had done, and
to keep the soldiers from getting any closer to the families.

Joseph had fought through that day beside his warriors,
and it was not until after dark that he found his wife. She
was with other women and their children in a rain-flooded
depression extending off the north coulee. They had not seen
each other since morning, when he left to send back pack

ponies, and her first question was of the elder daughter
who had gone with him.

Joseph could only shake his head. "I do not know. We
could see from the bluffs that the pack ponies and some of
our people got away. Later the soldiers chased them and
came back with ponies."

"Then they are all dead."

He placed a hand on her shoulder and turned away. The
day had cost him dearly, otherwise, although his warriors
had exacted five lives before they gave up one of their own.
He had lost four of his chiefs in those ferocious hours, men
who had bought with their blood the day's draw in the
battle.

On the north ridge Looking Glass, that old good friend of
his father and wise counselor of himself, had fallen with a
bullet through his forehead. Poker Joe had also died in that
bitter struggle for the heights, and down in the west coulee,
where even fiercer fighting had been, his half-brother, Ollicut, had died and with him old Tuhulhutsut, the medicine
chief whose *wyakin* at last had failed him.

Yet he still had Yellow Bull and the unrelenting White
Bird to help him, and their position had proved itself too
strong for the soldiers to carry. The coulees interjoined and
communication was easy, and after nightfall, while the warriors sniped at the encircling soldiers, the women and old
men began to strengthen their position even more. Rifle pits
were dug and fortified in yet other places, and they were
connected by trenches with the coulees. Dugouts were
gouged in the banks to shelter the wounded and weak.
Others left the trenches and crawled to the village to come
back with what food, blankets, and buffalo robes they could
find.

The snow fell thicker, the cold deepened, but there could

be no fires. Gun shots crackled like popping corn through which came the low wails of the women for the dead and the crying of half-frozen children. Joseph found White Bird in the north coulee where the young chief, with less than fifty warriors, was holding off four times his number on the bluffs.

"You have done well," Joseph said. "Even these new soldiers, wherever they came from, could not get past you today. But I have even more to ask of you. I want six of your best young men."

White Bird's voice seemed to come from rusty lungs. "You want them to slip past the soldiers?"

"Yes. I want them, or as many as can get away, to go to Sitting Bull. Our other runners only told him we are coming. These must say we have been attacked, that he must come and help us before the soldiers of the one-arm are on us too."

"The Sioux!" White Bird said contemptuously. "They are like the Crows, for we fought them today. This morning I saw one kill a woman who was after a pony. It was one of them who killed Looking Glass, I was told."

"I know. They are traitors, just as Nez Percés were traitors back in our old home. But the Sioux with Sitting Bull are different. They are men as we are men."

"I will do it," White Bird agreed.

CHAPTER SEVENTEEN

TWILIGHT AT NOON

Morning brought a high wind that came scouring from the north and poured through the draws and went washing over the flat. During the night some of the women had ventured forth to dig in the snow with numbed hands and feet, hoping to find buried buffalo chips. They had been partly successful, and now they were in a shallow depression a little apart from the trenches, risking shots from the soldiers and the big gun on the bluffs by building fires to provide hot food for their families and the wounded. While they were doing this, a shell lobbed in on them and killed two women and a girl, burying several more.

Out in the west coulee, Yellow Bull looked out through the screening sage to see snow-dust fly in the air and sweeping drifts drape their pleats over the naked country. He had been in this shot-ripped coulee for twenty-four straight hours and was no longer a young man, and his bones ached with weariness while his empty belly lay flat and complaining. Like his warriors, he had stripped for action when the shooting started. Now there was no retrieving the clothing he had discarded and no hope of getting a blanket for his tired shoulders, which were puckered from the piercing cold.

He was taking this look when the call of a bugle knifed through the sifting snow, the tones sharpened by the intense cold, and bounced along the hills.

He did not understand the connection, but the shooting everywhere about the camp broke off immediately. It dawned on him presently that the soldier chief had ordered this, which astonished him. His position was nearest to the sheltered draw where the soldier chief had set up head-quarters, and only the corner of the western flat intervened, bounded by the coulee his warriors held and the deep trench of Snake Creek.

His keen eyes drilled into the milky distance, and he saw an enemy Indian move forward with a white flag, the mean-ing of which was clear to him. The Indian, either a Sioux or Cheyenne, came on to within calling distance of the coulee and began to shout something in a strange tongue. It was Chinook jargon, with which the Nez Percés were none too familiar, but a warrior watching at Yellow Bull's side knew enough of it to prick up his ears.

"I think he says," the warrior muttered, "that the soldier chief would like to see Joseph."

"What is this, now?" Yellow Bull wondered aloud. "Ask him what for."

There was more shouting, and presently the interpreter turned to Yellow Bull again. "The name of the new soldier chief is Miles, he says, and they do not want to kill any more of our people."

"Our people?" Yellow Bull said with a snort. "They do not want us to kill any more of theirs. They cannot stand the bleeding and dying, not even the cold. Pah! They are old women."

"He says they will not shoot any more if Joseph will come over and talk."

Yellow Bull considered that for a moment, then slipped off along the coulee to find the war chief, to whom he reported what the enemy Indian had said. "It is a trick," he concluded. "We do not know this Miles, but they all speak with forked tongues. If you place yourself in their hands, they will shoot you so we will no longer have you to lead us."

Joseph shared that distrust, yet the soldier chief's offer had weight with him. His people needed a respite, a chance for the women to cook warm food without drawing gunfire. But perhaps he could gain that by temporizing, so he said, "Tell them the offer was not expected. I will have to think about it."

Yellow Bull nodded and hurried back to the coulee, and shouts rang over the flat, and the ceasefire continued. Smoke of chip fires went fraying off on the wind, but the soldier chief proved too wily to allow a rest that brought him no benefit.

This time two Indians who could speak the Nez Percé tongue came with a white flag and continued clear across to the coulee. Yellow Bull sent for Joseph, who went to talk with them. They told him that they were Indians too, and understood his fears, but they believed that Miles had their best interests at heart and could be trusted more than most of the government's head men. Miles thought that if things were talked over in a friendly spirit, they said, an agreement might be reached that would end the fighting. Finally, they warned, Joseph must come to Miles at once or the shooting would be resumed immediately.

"I will go, then," Joseph said without hesitation. It was the only way to get warm food for his people and a little time for them to rest.

Miles was watching across the flat when he saw the big, half-naked Nez Percé come up from the coulee with the two Cheyennes. Since he was shivering even in a bearskin coat, he felt a surge of admiration for the Indian's stoicism. He was not deceived that Joseph was in a mood to surrender, but the ceasefire had been attractive to him, and that looked hopeful. Miles walked forward to meet the party and held out his hand to Joseph and felt the impact of the large brown eyes that stared deeply into his own. The Nez Percé was too wary to accept the hand which, if taken, would be a pledge of friendship he would have to honor.

For the first time Joseph spoke directly to an enemy in English, saying, "You see that I have come. What do you want of me?"

"For the sake of your people," Miles said gently, "I want you to surrender. You know General Howard, and he is coming and will be here very soon. With him is the soldier chief you fought on the Yellowstone, Colonel Sturgis. They are bringing three times the soldiers I now have around you. You know you are surrounded and cannot escape, even from me. Perhaps you hope for help from the outlaw Sioux, but have any other Indians lifted a hand on your behalf? Will Sitting Bull?"

These arguments were shrewdly sound, and they were cogent with the Nez Percé. After a moment Joseph said gruffly, "If I surrender my people, what will happen to them?"

"It must be unconditional, whatever the white chiefs in Washington say."

Joseph's answer was to turn on his heel, and Miles said sharply, "Wait! You must not continue this hopeless war! Look!"

Swinging back, Joseph saw the rifles of nearby soldiers trained on him. In a hollow voice he said, "It is as we thought it would be. Your truce was a lie."

"I've got to end this senseless slaughter," Miles said earnestly. "Without you your people would quit. I'm going to hold you until you agree or the other soldiers come and you see for yourself how hopeless your cause is."

"Treachery."

"Call it that if you like, but I'm only hoping to save lives."

Yellow Bull and the watching warriors saw their chief's

angry motions and the rifles leveled on him by the soldiers. Growls broke from their throats, and their own weapons sprang into position.

"No," Yellow Bull said emphatically. "They would only kill him."

And so through that freezing day the ceasefire continued, uneasily and in deep distrust. In late afternoon Miles' wagon train came in, fighting its way through the drifts, and there were medical supplies, tents and blankets for the wounded, and food and ammunition for the troops. The snowfall kept up and it fell also on General O. O. Howard who that evening reached the Missouri River town of Carroll with two aides, a scout, seventeen men, and two treaty-Nez Percés. They had come ahead of the oncoming command in an effort to make contact with Miles, from whom Howard had heard nothing as yet.

Sheltered finally by a tent for his headquarters, Miles waited for the end to come. If anything, the approaching night threatened to be colder still. Yet it came on without any feelers coming from Joseph's subchiefs, who now were deprived of the fertile and daring brain that had led them so skillfully to this point. Deep in the colonel's heart was a sense of guilt over the way he had brought about the truce. Even though the reason had been humane, it bothered him, and surely it had brought no change of attitude to the prisoner he now held.

Just the same, with the train on hand, he could offer food and permission for the band to gather its possessions and return to the bullet-riddled teepees if they would but lay down their arms. He preferred to receive an emissary from them but when none arrived he sent for one of his most daring young officers, Lovell H. Jerome.

"This isn't an order, Lieutenant," he said, "but if you care to undertake it, it might hurry things along. They won't trust another flag of truce, but I'd like to get word to the Indians that they can share everything we have if they will surrender their weapons."

"How, sir?" Jerome asked.

"Most of the families are in those washes where we've seen smoke today. If you could talk to the women they might listen, if only for the sake of the children. And certainly they can do more to persuade the warriors to give up than we can."

"What if none of them speak English?"

"Most of them do and will when it suits their purpose."

"I'll have a try at it, Colonel.'

"Good. I'd say to take a horse and circle the position and come in on the northwest."

"I'll do my best."

Miles shook the young officer's hand, and Jerome donned his great coat, while a private brought up his horse. Mounting, he started out through the storm, hunched against the wind and dropping down the creek to cross and circle back. The blinding storm betrayed him when he came in on the field again, for he rode directly into the coulee occupied by Yellow Bull and his warriors who promptly seized him.

Thus Miles received the emissary he had hoped for when Yellow Bull himself walked boldly through the lines to the command post. But the tired old chief had come to do the talking, not to listen, and he described Jerome's tan overcoat and black horse so accurately that Miles knew they had the lieutenant. When Joseph was returned to his people, Yellow Bull stated, the young officer would be returned to his command, and he insisted on seeing Joseph to be sure he had not been harmed. Before departing he dropped a hint that his warriors already wanted to kill the young officer and would not be contented to wait long to have their own leader returned to them.

There was no more will to surrender in the hostile camp than there was in Joseph, Miles realized, and at any moment the warriors might decide that their leader was lost to them, whether or not he was harmed, which would mean the lieutenant's death. Miles capitulated, and the next morning the prisoners were exchanged halfway between the lines.

The battle was resumed, a sniping deadlock in which the troops lay on the freezing ridges and in the rifle pits on the flat and got shot at every time they moved. They knew that neither side could obtain a decision without days more of this unless Howard or Sitting Bull arrived to swing the balance one way or the other.

On that day the courier Miles had dispatched reached Colonel Sturgis, who was bringing on the combined command. This was still south of the Missouri River, fighting its way through the drifts that continually stalled the train. Concurrently Howard, having taken a boat at Carroll and gone up to the Cow Island crossing, was making his typical plodding way toward the battlefield.

The next morning the snow dwindled to a gentle sifting, and visibility was fairly good again. Miles was occupied with the fighting he had tried so earnestly to end when a sentinel from an outpost down the creek came rushing to headquarters.

"Colonel!" he gasped, nearly out of breath. "Something's coming, and a lot of it—our way!"

"What's that?" Miles said sternly, shoving to his feet. "Where?"

"From the northeast."

The direction was wrong for it to be Howard or Sturgis. "Sitting Bull!" Miles said grimly. "Joseph's won his gamble!"

The prospect was horrifying, and he began to consider

how to swing from an offensive to a defensive posture and
what he could do to protect the wounded. Catching up his
field glasses, he strode out into the galling cold and mounted
the nearby butte. He soon located the vast, moving body,
what appeared to be a thousand horses, slowly flowing
across the great fields of snow. They were still a few miles
away, and he felt his heart contract while he studied the
picture.

To the amazement of the adjutant, who had come with
him, Miles began to laugh.

"What is it, Colonel?"

"Buffalo. Driven down by the storm."

"Thank God."

"Amen to that."

Although he could not see the specter that had so alarmed
Miles, Joseph clung to his hope that Sitting Bull would yet
come to help him. But White Bird had grown pessimistic.
"Eleven suns have passed," the young chief said, after the
fighting died down that night, "since you sent the first runners to him."

"It is the snow," Joseph said doggedly. "And he could be
living farther in the north than we thought."

"We are about out of shells," White Bird reminded him.
"The soldiers have plenty, and when they think we are weak
enough they will charge us. Then we will not be living if
the Sioux do come to help."

"What is in your mind about it?"

"We could get away in the darkness. Tonight."

Joseph shook his head. "Yes, we could escape if we left
our wounded, our old men and women and our children
behind. I am not willing to do that. Are you?"

White Bird grunted, but it was in agreement with what
Joseph had said.

So for another day the stalemated battle continued, the

opposed commanders each hoping for help that would tip
the scales. The weather cleared but remained frigid and
blustery, and the outcome was being decided far away from
the Bearpaws. Howard had remounted his party at the Cow
Island crossing and struck out on the snow-choked trail to
the north. Behind him came Sturgis, who had reached the
Missouri and was fording his force of nearly eight hundred
men. And north, over the border of Canada, Indian faithless-
ness was at work again.

The first runners, whom Joseph sent off to Sitting Bull
from Cow Island, had fallen into the hands of the Assini-
boins and been murdered for their rifles. Those dispatched
later and from the battlefield had fought their way through
the blizzard, day after bitter day, only to find that the Sioux
chief had learned through other sources of the Nez Percé
flight and the Army's pursuit. Instead of rushing gallantly
to help his red brothers, Sitting Bull had packed his village
and moved deeper into the north, dealing himself out of the
struggle.

On the evening of October the fourth, Howard and his
party of twenty-three reached the Bearpaws and saw
through the thickening dusk the flash of the angry guns. His
aides were Lieutenant C. E. S. Wood and the general's son,
Guy Howard. Miles rode out to meet them, accompanied
by his adjutant, an orderly, and three other enlisted men.
Miles saluted his superior who, by his arrival, had assumed
command, then the two officers shook hands.

"Miles, I'm glad to see you," Howard said jovially. "I was
afraid you might have met Gibbon's fate. Why didn't you
let me know?"

Miles glanced at him sharply but said nothing, then
escorted the party into the command post on the south side
of the battlefield. He ordered a tent prepared for Howard

and meanwhile took him to his own. To his disappointment he learned that Sturgis was still a day's march behind.

But the general was cheerful. "I think the threat will be enough to turn the tide," he said. "And I've brought a couple of Nez Percé who might have some influence with friend Joseph. They each have a daughter with him."

Miles shook his head doubtfully. "What kind of terms can you offer?"

"Unconditional surrender."

"I tried that. It only strengthened their resolve to fight it out."

"Blast it, they can't hope to win."

"They can hope to die as free men, sir. I'm afraid that's what they'll choose."

Howard's one hand stroked his wiry beard. He had covered some 1600 miles in pursuit of the Nez Percés over a period of three and a half months. He had suffered rebuke and scorn, while Joseph had won the grudging admiration of the entire nation. For the first time the Nez Percé chief was pinned down, surrounded, and soon to be overwhelmed. Yet it was a sad thing to have to kill him.

He said, "Well, we'll make the try in the morning."

In the cold, clear dawn a bugle sent another cease-fire ringing along the Bearpaws. Under a white flag Howard's two Nez Percés advanced toward the hostile lines. They were Old George and Captain John, reservation Indians who nonetheless had had their hearts torn by the war, their daughters being married to fugitive warriors. They were not fired upon, and as they came forward one called, "All my brothers, I am glad to see you alive this sun!"

There were murmurs of anger when the two were recognized, but wiser heads restrained this, and the emissaries were taken to Joseph. The Indians sensed that there had been some change, that something of moment impended. They gathered about, and Captain John, his old eyes searching for sight of his daughter, spoke to them.

The one-armed general had reached the field, he said. Before this sun was set his many hundreds of soldiers would be on hand, and there were already many soldiers all about this little flat. But the officers would give much not to have to fight any more. They could not promise anything except that there would be no punishment. The Indians would be given food and blankets, they could have fires again and medicines for their wounded and time to rest. Old George added his plea, saying he believed General Howard's heart was now good, that Miles was an honest man who had sent his personal wish to sit down again with Joseph and talk matters over.

"Go!" Joseph told them impatiently. "I have nothing to say to that!"

His words were endorsed by a stir among the warriors, yet on the faces of the women he saw disappointment, and his heart grew heavy as he watched the emissaries walk out across the snow. •

Midday passed, and Joseph still could not find peace in his heart. Some great changes had come upon the world. None of the Indians of Idaho, Oregon, and Washington had rallied to his cause. Only a few treaty Nez Percés had come off the reservation to join him, and the Crows had fought him and tried to steal his horses.

It seemed that the Indians everywhere had reached a point where, if they did not curry favor with the white people, they deemed it well not to antagonize them. He had not let himself believe that before, but now he faced it. So it must be with Sitting Bull, with everyone except this little band of Nez Percés, so that there was no help for them at all except as it lay in the Great Spirit who did not seem to favor them.

By nightfall there would be three times as many soldiers about this place. They would have not only more rifles but more cannon and Gatling guns. The ammunition of the Indians would be gone by another morning, their food was nearly exhausted. The warriors would fight to the death willingly, but he could not bear to see more suffering among the others. They had endured too much already.

He called the other chiefs to him and told them what lay so heavily on his heart. "Twice the soldier chiefs have asked for a truce," he concluded. "I have never asked to quit fighting."

"That is true," Yellow Bull agreed. "They can starve us. They can kill us. But they cannot whip us and they know that."

White Bird said, "What you do is all right with me."

"You will not surrender?"

"Never." The old fierceness rang in the young chief's voice. "Somehow I will get away with my warriors and go to the land of the red coats. But I will wait until you have done the best you can for our people."

Joseph turned to Yellow Bull. "Go to the soldier camp and tell their chiefs I will talk with them."

A sense of impendency had drifted around the battlefield, and the weary troops hoped earnestly that the end was near. The officers around the command post knew when the lone Indian came across the field that it could be. Their eyes brightened in hope when presently the ranking officers walked back across the frozen flat with the old Nez Percé and halted at the midway point, their staffs and guard forming behind them.

Standing with Howard, Miles glanced at his watch and

noted that it was 2:20 P.M. of the sixth day of the fighting when Joseph came out of the coulees, followed by his people, and something tightened in the colonel's throat. The Indians spread over the snow, many of them in bare feet, and the man who led them came forward and offered his rifle to Howard. The general shook his head gently and pointed to Miles.

Too moved to speak, Miles accepted the token of surrender. As he did so the warriors laid their own arms in the snow, and the dignity and tragedy of it kept the troops, who had raised out of their positions, from cheering. Joseph turned toward his people and lifted a hand.

His voice came from the weary depths of his heart when he explained why this had been done. Many of their warriors, their chiefs, and their people had been killed. The children were freezing to death. Some of their people had been cut off from them, and nobody knew where they were, how they fared. They had to have time and means to take care of their wounded, their children, to bury their dead, and unite what was left of their people. He had led them in war, had done his best, but as their leader he could offer them no less.

Turning to the south, he looked up toward the dark overcast, and his worn voice spoke again. "Hear me, my chiefs. I am tired. My heart is sick and sad. From where the sun now stands, I will fight no more, forever."

EPILOGUE

Crushingly conclusive as it seemed, nothing was settled in the freezing winds at Bearpaw Mountain. The hope of eventual justice did not die in the hearts of the Nez Percés, nor did the defiance subside in the blood of the young chiefs and warriors. Seven bitter years were passed before anything resembling a settlement came about, years that saw the ranks of the stalwarts further decimated.

True to his warning, young White Bird refused to recognize the surrender as binding upon himself and his band, and in the night after the capitulation escaped from the encampment. Joined with the segment cut off at the start of the battle, he made his way northward across the snows to Milk River at the head of a hundred invincibles. Only a third of them were warriors, and nearly all of these bore wounds.

North of the Milk they came upon Bois Brulés, half-breeds descended from Indian mothers and white fathers, who gave them food, clothing, blankets, and moccasins. Then on across the boundary into the land of the red coats trudged the pathetic little band to discover that Sitting Bull, on whom they had pinned their hopes for so long, had responded to the pleas of Joseph's messengers by pulling five hundred miles deeper into the north. On and on went the refugees, and when at last they found the renegade Sioux they were received more like prisoners than brothers in a common plight.

Meanwhile Joseph, Yellow Bull, and their bands had been

moved to Fort Keogh, where Tongue River came down into the Yellowstone. It was the earnest hope of Colonel Miles that he could return his captives to an Idaho reservation, if not to their native Wallowa, but at the end of the winter orders from Washington caused them to be moved in the opposite direction to Fort Lincoln at Bismarck, North Dakota. From there they were taken down the Missouri to Fort Leavenworth, Kansas, then on to Baxter Springs, Kansas, where they arrived in July 1878, to fall victim to malaria, malnutrition, heat, and heartbreak.

As spring broke that year, General O. O. Howard, who had returned to the Department of the Columbia, was presented with an unexpected repercussion of the campaign. Inspired by the near success of the Nez Percé rebellion, some eight hundred Bannocks under Buffalo Horn jumped the reservation at Fort Hall, in southeastern Idaho, to join with Piutes from Nevada for a drive up the Columbia to the border of Canada. Again the stubborn general was leading a column in dogging pursuit, while a wave of terror ran ahead of the swiftly moving hostiles.

The rustling of the leaves had already carried the word to the camp of Sitting Bull where it fired the hearts of no one but White Bird and his little band. These prepared at once to take the field and join the new rebels in the Columbia basin, where it was hoped that Moses, the renegade of that area, would likewise rise up in arms with the Yakima and Umatilla recalcitrants. The White Bird band slipped across the border and broke into halves, one of which moved directly west toward the Columbia under White Bird, the other going south to cross into Idaho by way of the Bitterroot Valley and the Elk City trail.

The uneasy military was soon aware of the movement without realizing that the returned Nez Percés had divided.

Concentrating on the band of twenty-four that slipped down the Missouri toward Helena, army and volunteer detachments succeeded only in breathing the Indians' dust until they were crossing the Bitterroots. There, on Clear Creek, Lieutenant Wallace and a detachment of Third Infantry from Fort Missoula succeeded in making contact for a short, ineffectual fight. Escaping unscathed, the Nez Percés managed to reach Lahmotta Canyon, where the first battle of the war had been fought, hoping to secure cached ammunition, money, and food. Meanwhile White Bird had made his way unmolested to the upper Columbia and turned south toward the Spokane.

Thus situated, word reached both parties that the cause was already lost. Buffalo Horn had been killed in a battle with volunteers at South Mountain, with the Bannocks not yet united with the Piutes. Under lesser leaders the hostiles had been overtaken again, not by trudging General Howard but by Captain Barnard of Fort Boise, and thoroughly threshed on Silver Creek, in southeastern Oregon. Chief Moses had shown no interest in throwing his forces into the fight, and the new uprising was over almost before it began.

White Bird's last hope was gone. None of them wanted to return to the unfriendly, apathetic Sioux in Canada, and they could not expect to live as renegades in the country from which they had been driven once before. Surrendering voluntarily to the military at Fort Lapwai, they were sent to join Joseph at far-off Baxter Springs.

There, for six more years, the Nez Percés remained, reduced in number from the original 450 to 280, forgotten by nearly everyone but Nelson A. Miles who later was to write: "The solemn pledge of 'from where the sun now stands I will fight no more,' taken by that natural prince of his race, was faithfully kept by Chief Joseph and his brave followers.

I exerted all possible influence to have the Nez Percés returned to their native country and to receive just and humane treatment; but, on the contrary, they were sent down the Missouri River to Kansas, camped for a time on the low marshy grounds near the river, and thence taken to the malarial district in the Indian Territory, where fifty per cent of their number died; and it was not until after years of urging and effort that I was able to have them sent back to Idaho, where the remnant of the tribe still remains."

But Joseph was not permitted to remain in Idaho, let alone to see the valley of the Wallowa that he loved. Sent to the Colville Reservation in northern Washington, he remained in exile until, on September 21, 1904, he fell dead before his teepee on the Nespelem, the heart that had borne so much worn out.